For Mary,
with heartfelt thanks
making my return to Ligonier
so precious.
   With love,
      Edna (Pistiner)

Song by the River

Song by the River

by

Edna Gerstner
(author of *Idelette* and *Jonathan and Sarah*)

Soli Deo Gloria Publications
...for instruction in righteousness...

Soli Deo Gloria Publications
P.O. Box 451, Morgan, PA 15064
(412) 221-1901/FAX 221-1902

*

Song by the River was published by Zondervan in 1960. This Soli Deo Gloria reprint is 1996. Printed in the USA. All rights reserved.

*

ISBN 1-57358-040-6

*

ACKNOWLEDGMENTS

For permission to use copyrighted material, grateful acknowledgment is made to the following:

To the author, Robert Aura Smith, for quotations from *Divided India*.
To the poet's son, for permission to use poes of Sir Rabindranath Tagore.
To Dodd, Mead, and Company for permission to quote lines from Sarojini Naidu and Laurence Hope

To my Family
"The lines are fallen unto me in pleasant places: yea, I have a goodly heritage."

PROLOGUE

THE JUNGLE ENDED ANGRILY where native scythes had managed to cut away a small clearing. It had been conquered but not subdued. Annually its crawling vegetation assaulted the small mud huts, the marble palace and the rice fields. Annually the more rugged of the villagers hacked it back to its own boundary in a fight for survival; both forest and man realized it was a battle to the death.

Across the rice fields from the clearing by the river, the jungle suffered an additional insult. Here on unholy ground, where no native would live, man had yet dared to build more permanently. There rambled a long brick bungalow, a square brick hospital, and a brick church whose tall brick spire challenged the tallest of the jungle trees.

The illustrious name of this jungle clearing — hardly worthy of any name — was *Surrak Annund,* Road to Joy. There was scarcely any road, and very little joy. The name of the river that flowed nearby was more appropriate. It was called *Rhota Nuddee,* the Weeping River.

The inhabitants of Surrak Annund on the Rhota Nuddee numbered in all one thousand souls. The Hindus claimed six hundred of them. The Mohammedans tenaciously held three hundred and fifty. The remainder, the minority as always, claimed to be the people of God. Of these Christians there were three Europeans.

In Surrak Annund, and with these three Europeans, our story begins and ends. They are Robert Townsend, his wife Marjorie, and Charis Brown — *Miss* Charis Brown.

CHAPTER 1

CHARIS BROWN EXAMINED HER HAND carefully under the bright arc light of the operating room. Then deliberately she took a needle, dipped it into alcohol, and pricked it deeply into the white patch on her palm. She did not flinch. She stared in horror at her hand. So absorbed was she that the opening and shutting of the operating room door did not startle her. It was only when the doctor reached her side that she jumped. Then she buried her hand guiltily against her white starched uniform, and turned a blanched face to him.

"Charis! Are you ill?" He started to take her arm, but she pulled away from him.

"Don't touch me!"

Seeing the wildness in her face he did not move. "Charis," he said gently, "what's wrong? Tell me. Please tell me."

She shuddered. "Robert. I am a leper." When he said nothing, only looked sadly at her, she thrust her whitened hand toward him. "See! I have a leprous spot on my palm. It has been there for days, growing steadily. Just now I plunged a needle deep into the flesh. The flesh is dead. I felt absolutely nothing."

Still he did not speak. Instead, he took her hand in his and turned the palm to face the light. There was a small whitened area in the center, but it was not leprous. He had not expected it to be.

His voice, when at last he spoke, was professional and brisk. "Charis, there is nothing here that even resembles leprosy."

"But I did not feel the needle. I did not feel the prick." Her voice faltered.

"You were so sure. You hypnotized yourself into feeling nothing. You know that can happen."

"Oh, Robert! Are you sure?" Her voice ached with her need for reassurance.

He turned to the table and sterilizing the needle she had left there, calmly plunged it into the flesh. This time she cried out at the cruel jab. It was a cry of pain, but also one of unspeakable relief.

Without looking at him again, she straightened her starched cap and walked out through the door into the hospital corridor. As Doctor Robert Townsend looked after her, the concern on his face had not lessened. Charis did not have leprosy, but this was the third contagious disease she had imagined herself possessing in the last six weeks. It looked much like the beginning of the end for Charis Brown.

Charis felt almost light-headed as she left the operating room. Reprieve again! She kept muttering, "Thank You, God, thank You, God," as she walked along the hospital corridor. Her friend and assistant nurse, Anugra Bai, came hurrying to her side.

"You are all right, Missahib?"

"Yes. Yes." She was still a little dazed. "Quite all right, Anugra Bai. Only tired, very tired. Could you take over for me now, please? I think I would like to take a walk before dinner."

"A *hawa khanna*—air eating—will do you good, Missahib-ji." But Charis seemed not even to hear her. She pushed open the heavy hospital doors, stepped outside and gulped greedy breaths of the hot parched air. The marigolds in the window boxes along the hospital veranda were an orange flame. She had never learned to like their musky perfume, but their color today cheered her. How her father had loved them — but then he had enjoyed everything Indian. She smiled, remembering him, and picked a small bouquet. She would walk to the Christian cemetery with them, and put them on his grave. It would be a long walk. It would do her good.

The Rhota Nuddee was low this evening. The rains had not yet come. She had read somewhere that ninety per cent of the country's rainfall came in June. Now in March the river was all but dried up. It flowed, deceptively small and quiet, almost a mile from its banks. Yet she knew by experience that once the monsoons broke, that small thread of a river would suddenly become a swelling torrent and would even break its banks. Every year the Rhota Nuddee's banks, upon which she walked, showed more and more erosion from the torrential times, the wearing effect of the tears of the Weeping River. But tonight the tiny stream flowed safe and far away and made no noise.

She passed the church her father had built. It still spoke for him, stretching its towers to God; but the roof, once so perfect with its lovely rust colored tiles, now showed, too, the erosion of the times. It was a constant struggle to keep things beautiful in this land. She found herself singing softly to herself, "Change and decay in all around I see: O Thou who changest not, abide with me."

She passed a group of labor women carrying their heavy loads on their heads. They were finishing for the day. She loved to watch their effortless walk, a graceful glide. Most of them did not even use a hand to steady their baskets filled to overflowing with heavy bricks. One woman stopped to speak to her, "Salaam, Missahib-ji." Deftly balancing her load of fifty bricks by the slightest sway of her body, she touched her hand to her forehead in the Indian form of greeting.

"Salaam, Ramquar. How are you? And how is the child?" She, too, touched the tips of the fingers of her right hand to her forehead just above the temple.

In answer the woman swayed her hips, and there tied snugly in a corner of her flowing sari lay her infant son whom Charis had delivered three weeks ago. Against all the rules of the book mother and son were doing well. Charis chuckled over the sweet brown baby, and chattered a while to the woman in her perfect Hindii, as native to her tongue as it was to Ramquar's. But she was glad when at last the woman went on her way and she was free to cross the flat *midan,* or field, alone to complete her pilgrimage.

The cemetery itself was a most depressing place. It had been located on the very edge of the jungle. Although the bodies were buried deep, jungle beasts — jackals for the most part — would creep in and tear up the ground in a frantic effort to reach the deceased. Somehow they always seemed to know when a funeral had taken place.

Charis used to stop her ears with her hands on those nights to shut out the mournful sound of their howling. And even as a child she had winced with every clod that had been thrown on the homemade wood coffins. Her eyes had always been fixed on the fringe of the jungle, feeling those animal eyes upon her. She had felt the horror of knowing that these carrion creatures were out there waiting to try to desecrate the bodies of those whom they buried.

When her father had died she had wanted to take up her watch at his grave like that great missionary of the New Hebrides, John G. Paton. She had read that he had lain across his wife's grave, musket in hand for ten days and ten nights, and guarded her grave aided only by his dog. His watch had been against the perverse cannibals of the island. He had left only when his wife's body was inedible. Her task would have been easier. She had only to keep watch against the soulless jungle beasts. She had not given in to her terrors, but the night her father had been buried, from the veranda she had seen a lantern burning in the graveyard, and for days no jackals howled. She would be eternally grateful to that unknown Christian who went against centuries of superstition to perform one last deed of devotion to his Sahib.

Two years had passed since her father's death, but it still hurt her to think of her gentle father buried in this place. Yet in all honesty she knew it was where he would have wanted to be. Even as David Livingstone had wanted his heart buried in his beloved Africa, her father had wanted his earthly tabernacle to become a part of the dust of his adopted land.

She walked through the rough mounds of graves until she found the one she had outlined with brick. Removing her nurse's cap she wiped the ever present dust away from the headstone. Andrew Brown, Missionary. 1875 - 1945. There had been no skilled hand to carve more than those words into the rough unhewn stone. She placed her small bouquet beneath the headstone, beside still another bouquet. She had never yet come to her father's grave without finding fresh flowers lying there. What loving hand, pagan or Christian, put them there she never knew. It was a lovely epitaph, far better than one of stone.

She found herself repeating the lines of a cinquain her father had written and which she had found, after his death, tucked away in the notebook in which he usually jotted much more practical items.

DAY'S END
God does
Not squander all
His talent on the dawn.
He saves His choicest colors for
Day's End.

The five short lines summed up his life. For her father's path had glowed from its beginning to its day's end with the reflected glory of heaven. But what was wrong with her? For her there was no radiance. It was as if in her case the smoking flax had been quenched, and the bruised reed broken.

She had never been a lighthearted girl. But this persistent depression and melancholy were new. Lately this deep sadness seemed to have become a permanent mood. She felt a vague longing eating deep within. Why was she depressed? Was her sorrow just that of the lonely heart? That of which the poet Goethe had written, *"Nur wer die Sehnsucht kennt, weiss, was ich leide . . ."?*

Softly she sang.

> None but the lonely heart
> Can know my sorrow,
> Alone and parted far
> From joy and gladness.
> Heaven's boundless arch I see
> Spread out above me.
> Ah! What a distance drear
> To one who loves me! . . .
> My senses fail,
> A burning fire devours me.
> None but the lonely heart
> Can know my sadness.

The jungle denseness muted her deep contralto voice. When the last sad bars of Tchaikovsky's music died away Charis buried her head in her hands and wept. Then with her hands still pressed hard against her face she prodded on with her self interrogation. "Or is my melancholy to be traced to a more specific cause, a more recent one? How much, Charis Brown," she asked herself, "do Robert and Marjorie have to contribute to your dejected state?"

But she shied away from her own direct question. She had engaged in introspection too long. She did too much thinking and talking to herself lately. Since Robert was no longer there to talk to . . . since Marjorie . . . . With summoned effort she buried her thoughts and made herself walk briskly to the bungalow. She must hurry and change for dinner. Marjorie would not like it if she appeared at the table in uniform.

CHAPTER 2

Robert's steps dragged as he walked across the brick veranda, through the screen door and into his *duftar*. He dropped wearily into his office chair and for a moment indulged his exhaustion, supporting his head in his hands. They still reeked of ether and disinfectant, and feeling a strong revulsion he walked over to the *surai* in the corner and poured out a handful of water and scoured them again. But even the lavender fragrance of the soap which Marjorie bought was no match for the hospital odor. He was not too tired to notice a symbolism in this fact. He did not dwell upon it, for he did not want to stir up in his weary mind his own muddled marital problems — not now. He did not even want to think back upon his pathetic interview with Charis Brown. In desperation he turned to the piles of mail accumulating dust on his desk.

It was amazing how here, miles away from civilization, the mails still managed to get through — how calamitous, really. He was the sole staff of the mission hospital, and with no secretarial help there were times when he would have liked to brush the accumulation into the waste basket. That is where ninety per cent of it belonged. Instead, he was always trying conscientiously to catch up on the *belighte dak* — the foreign mail — only to have himself engulfed, if he did succeed, with another deluge of correspondence. The jungle runner with the bells tied to his stick and his pouch bag full of mail was one of his biggest bugaboos. The jingling bells announcing the postman's arrival could be heard deep in the jungle and as the sound of the bells came closer he felt like taking to his heels along with the tigers and evil spirits they were supposed to exorcise from the runner's path.

He could not share the enthusiasm of the poet Kipling who had immortalized this foot-service in his poem "The Overland Mail." How did it go?

SONG BY THE RIVER

In the name of the Empress of India, make way,
O Lords of the Jungle, wherever you roam.
The woods are astir at the close of the day —
We exiles are waiting for letters from Home.
Let the robber retreat — let the tiger turn tail —
In the name of the Empress, the Overland Mail!
With a jingle of bells as the dusk gathers in,
He turns to the foot-path that heads up the hill —
The bags on his back and a cloth round his chin . . . .

He had forgotten the rest of the lines. He swiveled his chair around to his desk, and with grim determination opened the first letter on the stack. It was a mistake. It was from the mission board in America. It asked him confidentially to answer frankly and honestly whether he thought Miss Charis Brown should be returned to the field after her furlough which was due next January. He glanced through the questionnaire he was asked to complete. It contained the customary round of questions. "Does she get along with fellow workers? Is she a good psychological risk?" And finally, "Do you recommend her return?"

Now, of all days to get this. Ten major operations — two already septic — and now this! Reluctantly he pulled a blank sheet of foolscap paper toward him and forced himself academically to write up a case history on Charis Brown.

Age: Thirty-two.
Height: Five feet six inches.
Hair: Dark Brown.
Eyes: Brown.
Mental Capacity: Brilliant.
Devotion to Duty: Staggering.
Family: None. Mother died in childbirth. Father died of typhoid fever while in service on the field.
Capacity for Affection: Unlimited but untapped.
Present Health: Precarious.
Prescription: Facetiously he scrawled, "One husband, six children, and a bungalow preferably by a banyan tree."

He tore the sheet in two and then deliberately again and again until only scraps remained. There had been a time when he had been tempted to fulfill his own prescription. That was in the days when Marjorie, then his fiancée, had remained at home; and while maintaining that his God was her God, steadfastly refused to make his people her people. Charis had given him unasked her warm spontaneous sympathy and had seemed in turn to welcome his companionship. They had talked endlessly together. And there had been that evening by the Rhota Nuddee, when the sun had set and they had instantly been engulfed in the darkness of an India that knows no twilight, that he had been prompted by sheer propinquity and the moment to suggest they resolve their problems together.

It was Charis, now psychologically a poor risk, who had kept her head. In the soul searching of the present moment, why not be honest with himself? He wished, now, that she had not. What a mess he had made of things. Marjorie had come to India, but just lived for their return to the States. He knew that the natives, in their uncanny telepathic way, were already saying that the Doctor Sahib would not be with them long. Look at what his mad insistence had produced. He had cajoled Marjorie into missionary work, and she had become an unrecognizable and unlovely person. He had seen a Ruth in an Orpah.

And what of Charis? What had he done to this generous friend? How much of her conflict of the moment was his doing? If there had not been that moment by the Weeping River could he not have answered this telling question, "Do you recommend her return?" with a quick emphatic, "Yes."

And now the three of them were the only missionary workers of the Surrak Annund mission outpost. It would be a help if the mission board at home would avail itself for once of the wisdom of the world and see the dynamite latent in the situation. Even when he had requested a transfer to another mission hospital his request had been denied. Perhaps this second letter from the board was an outgrowth of that former request. Maybe some red-blooded member had read between the lines. Certainly if he now refused to recommend Charis' return it would resolve the situation. But his justness would not permit him to sacrifice her just because it was an easy solution. Should she return to the field? Could he give an objective answer? Would his answer be uninfluenced by his own tangled emotions? Certainly not this evening. He pushed the letter back on the pile.

What he should do was write the board at home frankly that it was possible for that "eternal triangle" to creep even onto the hallowed ground of a mission compound. It would jolt them back on their heels. It might even mean his recall. This would not keep him from writing; but what stopped his pen was that he could not do so without baring the disillusionment he had found in his marriage. This he could not bring himself to do so. Loyalty was too much a part of him. He hoped daily he could find another way. So he continued to pray, "Lead us not into temptation," and meanwhile circumstances forced him to walk a tightrope over the abyss.

CHAPTER 3

MARJORIE TOWNSEND SAT BEFORE her dressing table and with great care examined her eyes. Customs were strange. Here in India the women spent hours outlining their eyes with kohl. They even used belladonna, Robert had told her, to dilate the pupils to make them look larger. But they used all their art on their eyes. Even the red caste mark between the eyes only served to call attention to them. Perhaps it was as well, for their lips were thick, and their teeth usually black with decay. She smiled artificially at herself and took satisfaction in her lovely mouth, and the straight row of white teeth she possessed.

There was little in the mirror that would dissatisfy any woman. Her eyes were a deep blue, and her hair a golden bronze which seemed to frame artlessly a perfect oval face. Her hair had the slightest natural wave and with studied skill she managed to make it a perfect setting for her exquisite little face. She wore deep curled bangs across her forehead and let the rest fall carelessly in a page boy style about her shoulders.

She took one hand and fluffed her hair to one side. *Charis Brown,* she suddenly thought, *should do something about herself. She has a good profile, but who would notice it when her hair always looks as if she had just had a tight unset permanent? I wonder if she is worldly enough to use curlers, or is that tight curl natural? In any case it should be waved back from her forehead, and if that were done her lovely classic profile would demand attention. I'd like to get my hands on her.*

But after all, what would be the use? No one would ever see anyone buried in this hole in the jungle, anyway, she thought bitterly. Why couldn't Robert have been given a city hospital? Then at least she would have had some European companionship. This place was just a whistle stop for buffalo carts, and

SONG BY THE RIVER 17

by the time their furlough would be due she would be positively old.

There was absolutely nothing to do here. She dutifully took her Hindii lessons with the *Babu* and was learning to write her letters with a quill pen. She liked artistic work, and he had been delighted with her skill. But after he had gone there was nothing left to challenge her interest. Robert was at the hospital all day long. She could not speak to a soul except monosyllabically like a baby, for no one around the bungalow could speak English.

She could not even cook, for there was already a cook. She could not even plan his menus for him, for although he dutifully consulted her every day, he continued to serve what he had always done, curry and rice. The saffron smell of the sauce always turned her stomach. And she was deathly sick of rice. She remembered, with sympathy, the American soldier who had been terrified at the thought of capture by the Japanese — not dreading any torture that they could inflict — but as he had so pathetically explained, "I can't stand rice."

If she wanted to take a swim, the Weeping River was impossible. Occasionally a crocodile drifted down from up river. And she had nearly drowned of fright the last dip she had taken when she saw swimming along smoothly beside her some species of water snake. They had a tennis court, but Robert was always promising her a game another day.

Lately her situation had been getting worse. What had started as a strain between Robert and herself was now a deep rift. She knew she nagged him whenever she saw him. He had withdrawn from her into a defensive silence. Their marriage had reached the stage of a cold war.

What had happened to that delirious joy they had once found in each other? At college Robert had been everything a girl desired. He had been captain of the football team, president of the senior class, the man voted most likely to succeed. As a freshman she had been delighted when he had singled her out for his attention. In fact, she had been the envy of all the girls and had floated on pink clouds all that year. Even when he was graduated ahead of her his medical school was close enough for him to come down for college activities. She had loved going with an older man.

It was not until he was in his last year of medical school,

and she was already wearing his ring, that he told her of his desire to be a medical missionary. She was a Christian — after all her father was an elder in the church, and her mother had always taught a Sunday school class — but she thought Robert had gone mad.

They had fought about it all through his internship, and the engagement had been broken more than once. She had tried to fall in love with someone else, but Robert had a quality that drew her to him, and would not let her go. He had even gone to India by himself. It was she, finally, who capitulated. She had gone back to college Homecoming Week, and her memories had been her undoing. She had simply cabled him, "Unconditional Surrender."

The weeks of preparation, the farewell parties, even the long lovely ocean voyage — none of these had prepared her for India. As she came down the gangplank she was surrounded by the smell of the Orient — the sweaty bodies of unwashed coolies, open sewage and the peculiar stench of a land that ignores latrines.

Robert had been there to meet her and had thrown a lei of jasmine about her neck. He had looked wonderfully happy, tanned and virile. He at least was the same. But a part of her knew she had made a mistake, even in the security of his arms and with the fragrance of jasmine temporarily drowning all others.

As they had plowed through the masses of people on the dock Robert had explained to her that although India was only three-fifths the size of the United States, its population was more than that of North and South America and Africa combined. It had seemed to her then, and it had not changed, that India was one moving mass of humanity, most of whom it seemed pressed smotheringly around her. She, who had always loved a crowd, had now almost developed claustrophobia around people.

If only they could have had a honeymoon! Instead, Robert felt he had already taken too much time away from the hospital. That seemed to set the pace for their marriage. After a brief ceremony at the American mission — she hadn't even taken time to unpack her wedding dress — they had taken the long dusty train trip to Surrak Annund. Her wedding dress still lay in its original folds. Robert had never seen it. She was too proud now to even let him see her hurt, to let him know that she had bought one.

Although the strain had started early, the major break in their relationship had not come until one day Charis Brown had developed what she had feared was a case of typhoid. Robert had turned to her to give emergency help in the hospital. She knew he needed her, but she could not make herself go into the wards and nurse these people. She had always hated nursing. "A nurse's job," Robert, the intern, had himself once told her, "is about seventy per cent charmaid chores." How could she bathe those bodies? She had heard Robert and Charis discussing the fact that only Christian natives went in for nursing, for the Hindu girls felt the work defiled them. She was one with them in this sentiment. She had refused her help and her husband had not only been disappointed, he had been sharp with her about her attitude.

She in turn had become angry. She had failed to take into account the urgency of the situation, his extreme fatigue, and she had driven him from her with recriminations. She had said a great many things she did not mean about him and about his work.

In the intervening days he had not forgiven nor forgotten her words. Since then the strain between them had been growing steadily worse. She was always saying ill-tempered, vicious things. *I hate myself for it. But I hate him, too. We must get away from this place. It is tearing us apart. If I can only divorce Robert from his work I'm sure everything will be all right again,* she thought with childish optimism. Gently she touched the new dark circles which were beginning to show under her eyes. *And I think I have the weapon with which to do it.*

The brass dinner gong sounded. Standing and smoothing her powder blue voile, she pushed aside the bead curtains to join the others in the dining room. Even at dinnertime Robert and she were not alone. There were the servants, and always eating with them was Charis Brown.

CHAPTER 4

THE DINING ROOM WAS LOCATED in the center of the long brick bungalow. Adjacent to it in the central wing and divided from it by an open archway was the sitting room. Radiating from these two central rooms on each side were two identical apartments, consisting of three large rooms and a bathroom. Along both sides of the house ran a wide roofed-in veranda.

The Townsends occupied one of these apartments and Charis Brown the other. The room closest to the dining room in the Townsend half was used by Robert for his office.

The floors of all the rooms were of concrete, and the ceilings were high. In the central wing they were thirty feet from the floor; they sloped slightly at each end of the house. Set high in the wall were small windows which were opened and shut by ropes which hung to the floor. Then at waist level each room had long wide windows. In the hot weather from dawn to sunset each day all the windows were closed; and the high walls, the cool floors and the rattan furniture all helped to make the house bearable.

But the most vital piece of furniture was the *punkha* or fan. Over and across the center of each room was this wide matting. It was attached to a long solid wooden pole from the center of which a rope extended straight across to the outside wall and through a small hole. Outside, on the veranda, the end of the rope was tied to the wall unless it was being used by the *punkha walla* or fan puller.

This March evening it was unbearably hot, and as Marjorie stepped into the dining room she was glad to see the *punkha* drifting slowly back and forth across the room giving a soft breeze. Outside a small brown boy sat. While singing softly, rhythmically, he pulled the rope as one tolls a bell. Robert was in a corner of the dining room pumping up the pressure kerosene lamp. With the usual perversity of inanimate objects it was refusing to light.

"Are you out of kerosene?" Marjorie asked. It was a typical woman's solution, and Robert looked his reply. He picked up the light to shake it and show her her folly. Instead, his face reddened. It was quite obvious to them all that the container was empty. It did not help his disposition to have her add sweetly, "Let it go, Robert. It is more romantic anyway to eat by old-fashioned lamplight."

She went back into their quarters to bring their lamp. Charis contributed hers, and it was in this subdued light that the dinner was served. Dhunwa, the cook, appeared in a clean white chef's coat. He looked antiseptic and immaculate. It was hard to realize at these moments that this was the same Dhunwa who invariably dried the dishes with his shirt tail, and whom she had caught toasting the bread between his toes before the open fire. It was just as well to forget it.

With skill he helped Marjorie to a heaping service of rice. "May I not give Memsahib-ji a little curry tonight? Very good." His voice coaxed.

She shuddered, "No. No thank you, Dhunwa." She had offended him now. This had all the earmarks of another of those evenings.

"Robert," said Charis brightly, "have you had time to read *Divided India* by Robert Smith?"

No one, of course, would assume that she ever read anything but the funnies, Marjorie thought bitterly.

"No. Tell us about it," replied her husband.

"I found him most enlightening on the subject of home rule or *Swa-raj*," Charis continued.

"Did you?" Robert was interested. Marjorie was not, and began to weave her own thoughts while the conversation flowed past her.

"Does he favor a divided India and the creation of an independent Mohammedan state?" Robert asked.

Charis thought a moment. "He is objective. I don't recall him favoring any one position. I think he merely poses the problem. He does this well. He sums up all the political party views succinctly, each in a sentence. Very catchy, I thought. For example he says the Hindus feel that the British should *Quit India First.*"

"I usually mistrust any glib sentence summarizations," interjected Robert, "but that isn't bad. A Hindu friend of mine once said, 'The British must leave and let us work out our own solution. Home rule will be a headache. But are we not entitled to our own headaches?'"

"Ghandi was quoted recently," said Charis, "as saying, 'If we are left to ourselves we will readily find a way. Some people call that anarchy. I prefer to call it God.'"

We're off, groaned Marjorie inwardly, *to another intellectual evening.*

"For the Muslims," Charis continued, "the slogan he gives is *Split India First.*"

"I agree again," said Robert. "In spite of their background of Moghul rule, the Mohammedans of today are afraid of a United India. They are conscious of being greatly outnumbered — eighty-four million to almost four hundred million. Even in the Indian Army where you would expect them to be in the majority they are thirty-two per cent of that body over against a Hindu forty-seven per cent. The remaining percentage is Christian, Sikh and Ghurka. I heard one military man appraise the situation by saying a Civil War in India would last ten years and result in a Hindu victory. I believe the Mohammedans would say *Split India First.*"

"Choudhary Rahmat Ali has coined a clever name for the new Mohammedan State," Charis added. "Pakistan, he would have it called. It sounds like Pukhastan, meaning a good solid state — a good enough name; but actually each letter stands for a geographical entity of the new country. *P* stands for the *Punjab,* a fertile province which lies within the boundary of Pakistan. *A* stands for the large and powerful country of *Afghanistan* which borders Pakistan on the northwest. *K* stands for the beautiful country of *Kashmir,* sometimes called the Switzerland of India, which borders Pakistan on the northeast. *I* stands for the *Indus* River which flows through the land. *S* stands for the desert province of the *Sind.* This is the other province which lies within the boundary lines of Pakistan. And, finally, *TAN* stands for another country, *Baluchistan,* a warlike state which borders Pakistan on the west."

"Do you favor a divided India, Charis?" Robert asked.

"I hate to see India mutilated, a corner chopped away. And yet, Robert, one has to be practical; and with the feeling running as high as it does between the Hindus and the Mohammedans no other solution promises to my mind much peace."

"And yet, wasn't it Akbar the Great, himself a Moslem, who governed India and permitted religious freedom? I understand he would deliberately wear Hindu religious marks on his forehead and also wore the sacred girdle of the Zoroastrians."

"Could you then call him a Moslem?"

Robert granted her the point. It was always a pleasure to talk with Charis. Her mind always offered a challenge and stimulus to his own.

"How does Smith feel we will fare, we who live under an Indian Rajah? There are, I believe, 562 independencies in India governed by native princes. How do the princes feel?"

"He uses this sentence for them, *Guarantee Our Tenure First.*"

Robert made no comment. "And finally," Charis concluded with a smile, "as you would expect, he paints a charitable British picture by giving them the slogan, *Reach an Agreement and Draft a Constitution First.* So, in the end, even the British Lion believes in *Swa-raj.*"

"Charis, are you pro-British?" Robert suddenly asked.

"Yes, I am. I know Britain failed in the early days, failed even Christian missions; and I am not blind to her early exploitation of this country. As Winston Churchill once pointed out, at one time 'One person in five in the United Kingdom derived his livelihood from India.' But not today. It is just the opposite. India has now become an economic liability. If not earlier, it is now what Kipling calls the 'White Man's Burden.' And I feel that Britain is shouldering that burden well."

Robert gave her a quizzical look, and she rushed on in her defense. "Take just legislation, for example. Think of the humane laws that have been passed in the century of British rule. Abolishment of Child Marriage by the Sarda Act, and the outlawing of *Suttee* (widow suicide), are just two such instances. And to pass these you know how much orthodox Hindu opposition had to be overcome. When *Suttee* was outlawed a group of Orthodox Hindus went to London to protest Great Britain's interference in matters of religion. Whatever their past record, certainly in my lifetime the British government has been behind every decent and good law that has been passed."

"And now let's turn the page of history to the Amritsar Incident." Robert's tone was sharp for him.

"You must remember what preceded that massacre, Robert. There had been a number of innocent white residents butchered. One British woman missionary had been hacked to bits on a busy city street by an enraged mob. General Dyer then passed an order, I understand, that no Indian could ever again walk down that street. Every native had to crawl on hands and knees. And an order was passed forbidding any public meetings or any gathering of more than four people.

"Yet at four o'clock in the afternoon of the day of the Amritsar Incident, at Jallianwal Bagh, a great crowd gathered. General Dyer came with fifty riflemen. Three times he gave the order to disperse. It was only then, after his orders had been ignored, that he had his soldiers open up with machine guns."

"There were about six thousand people in that square," Robert interrupted, "four hundred were killed and one thousand wounded . . . ."

"But Robert," Charis urged, "you must admit the mutiny was stopped. Many people feel if General Dyer had not shown a strong arm this country would have blazed into another horrible *Indian Mutiny*. Any force is justified to prevent that recurrence."

"Any force, Charis? He fired into an unarmed mob."

"They had butchered women and children."

"So he killed four hundred of them for a handful of whites to set the balance of justice straight . . . ."

"Will you please excuse me?" In obvious distress Charis broke into tears, rose and left the table.

It was an awkward moment. "Will you go bring her back this time or shall I?" asked Marjorie. "There is rice pudding for dessert. It would be a shame to miss it."

"Charis is ill." Robert's voice was ice. "She is not merely acting like a spoiled child out of pique. I don't know what possessed me to get on such a controversial subject tonight. It was unforgivable. Charis needs help, our help. She needs affection desperately. Marjorie, please show her a little warmth."

"Why, dear, when you do it so well?" She replied acidly.

The bead curtains tinkled as Charis stepped back into the room. "I'm sorry. Please forgive me. I haven't been myself

SONG BY THE RIVER

lately. I seem to be unable to talk on any subject dispassionately."

When Marjorie maintained her silence Robert felt called upon to answer. "It is a subject upon which few can keep a calm head these days."

Charis looked gratefully at him, then turning to his wife said, "Marjorie, how do you feel about *Swa-raj?*"

"I beg your pardon. Were you asking my opinion?" The delicately underlined surprise in Marjorie's voice at being finally addressed was deliberate and obvious.

Flushing, Robert tried to front for his wife. "Marjorie is hardly entitled yet to an opinion. India is still new and strange to her."

His explanation satisfied Charis. She failed to see the look that passed from Robert to his wife. And so the meal continued by lamplight in peace and silence.

CHAPTER 5

As THEY WERE RISING from the table they heard the voice of the *chowkidar* — night watchman — challenging someone in the compound. The *chowkidar* always energetically discharged his duties early in the evening; it was only after midnight that his snores added their peculiar contribution to the noises of the night.

He came into the dining room accompanied by a Hindu man. They could tell by his *chungri* that he was a Hindu. Many of them wore this long plait of hair on an otherwise shaved scalp; for superstition made them believe that they could be yanked to heaven by this strand. Hence it was never cut.

The man was covered with sweat; he had evidently been running a long distance. Sighting Charis, he turned to her and babbled in the district dialect. Robert never ceased to be amazed at how Charis spoke this foreign language. He kept forgetting it was her mother tongue.

"This man says his brother sent him to get medical aid for his wife. She is in labor and the child is not being born. They want me to go," Charis translated.

"Could I go?" Robert offered. "It is late at night. You should not be going down to the village now."

"You know that they would never permit you to attend her, Robert. Their taboos against a man doctor are still too strong. I wish — how I wish — you would be allowed. It sounds like a serious delivery case to me. It usually is when they call for me. I am," she said sadly, "too often a last resort."

"May I go with you?" Marjorie asked.

Both Robert and Charis showed their amazement. "Well, I can at least hold a lantern," she added.

When Robert said nothing, Charis spoke, "This delivery is not a good one for the uninitiated to see. It will most certainly not be a normal one. If you want to see a childbirth, Marjorie, why not wait until a baby is delivered in the hospital? It will give you a much more average picture of the process."

"At the rate Robert is attracting obstetrical cases," Marjorie replied, "it looks as if the first baby to be delivered there will be his own. You see, I shall be having a child myself in November, so I have a personal interest in wanting to go tonight."

Marjorie was sorry the moment she had spoken. She had meant to startle and hurt Robert by a public announcement of a fact of which he was still unaware. As usual, her words backfired. Her husband did not satisfy her by showing the slightest surprise at the announcement. Instead he said calmly, "I advise you strongly, Marjorie, to stay home."

"Do you speak as my physician or as my husband?" she asked pertly.

"As your doctor. Purely a medical opinion." His voice was sarcastic.

"Well then, Charis, I shall go."

"Marjorie, please — "

"Let her go," Robert said. Marjorie left the room to fetch her lantern.

Charis turned to the doctor, "Please keep her home, Robert. I am almost certain to lose this case. It is no sight for her to see . . . ."

"And what about you? Is it a sight for your eyes? Why should Marjorie be spared what you must see?"

"I was thinking about her condition. After all, I am not carrying your child . . . ." The words hung there between them. Charis felt awkward and was glad that at that moment Marjorie returned.

The women left immediately, with Marjorie in high spirits. Robert stood on the veranda and watched them until the lanterns they carried disappeared across the rice fields which separated them from the native *pahara*.

How like her, he thought bitterly of his wife, *to spoil even this moment for me.* And he could feel nothing but a weary numbness at the thought of the new life she had promised him.

CHAPTER 6

THE HUT THEY ENTERED was made of mud and was scarcely shoulder high. It had no windows and was covered and all but concealed by a low-hung thatched roof. As the two women groped through the doorway they were deafened by the furious beat of a native drum. When their eyes had stopped smarting from the dense smoke that oozed from a small native *chula*, they saw a drummer sitting in the doorway. He struck his tom-toms with a frantic rhythm, more wild with each beat. At intervals he would punctuate his notes with an eerie shriek.

On a matting on the floor in the far corner of the room lay the patient. She was foaming from the mouth in convulsion. Beside her sat an old hag, rubbing cow manure, whenever she could, on the tautly stretched skin of the writhing body.

The emotion that Marjorie felt uppermost was fear. It seemed an overpowering concentration of evil was in this hut. Then Charis took control, and the evil fled. Gently she usurped the place of the old granny without hurting her feelings. Even the drummer was ousted. Outdoors his drums could still be heard, but without causing the blood to pound from one's head. Marjorie went to stand beside Charis, and she held the light over the patient for her. A feeling of compassion, strange to her, stirred and was born within her. Ashamed now for coming here from foolish motives, she felt proud of her insignificant role.

As Charis expertly examined the patient, she explained to Marjorie, "The only medications these poor people know are fire, noise and cow dung. When they are ill they always make the sickroom as hot as possible. Sometimes they even apply hot pokers to the sufferer's flesh. Noise is always an accompaniment. You see, all illness to them is demon possession. So the cure is to exorcise the demon, and fire and noise are the best weapons they know. As for the cow manure, the cow is their sacred animal, and any of its excretions are priceless to them. Its application is supposed to be the piece de resistance. I'm afraid that the combination in this case will prove fatal — that plus the long delay before calling me."

Then she prayed simply, "O God, help me."

The lantern shook in Marjorie's hand. An overpowering lassitude took possession of her and with no warning she crumpled down on the mud floor.

When Marjorie regained consciousness the oppressive heat was gone. Looking about her she saw that she was in another mud hut, but there was no fire. The lantern's light showed her that she lay on a stringed native cot. The floor was swept clean. And looking down at her from the wall was a compassionate representation of the face of Jesus. She recognized the picture as one coming from the large sheets they used in the Sunday school. Her fear, her oppressive panic, she realized, had gone.

She stirred and a native woman came from the open door and held a brass drinking vessel filled with cool water to her lips. When she hesitated, she heard the woman say "Boiled, yes," repeating the strange words with difficulty, and gratefully Marjorie drained the cup. She recognized the woman as one of the Christian community, but she still did not know where she was or how she had been brought here. Someone must have carried her. She hoped Charis had not been burdened with her.

She wanted to ask about the patient, but found herself helpless with her meager Hindii vocabulary. Most of all, she realized, with a sweet sorrow, she wanted Robert. It had been too long since she had turned to him.

"Sahib, Sahib," she kept repeating to the woman.

And the woman smiled and nodded and went away. She must have dozed, for a gentle hand on her shoulder awakened her. The woman must have understood her desire for her husband for there in the doorway stood Robert. She had sent for him.

"Robert," her voice was weak.

He came quickly to her side, and knelt beside the cot. His face was a professional mask. She felt his strong fingers on her wrist as he took her pulse.

"It was hot, so very hot," she mumbled.

"You'll be all right, Marjorie. It was just a faint. Don't lift your head, and lie still." It was pleasant having Robert care for her.

"Where is Charis?" he asked.

"I don't know." She was ashamed to let him know of how little help she had been. As if in answer to his question, Charis stepped through the doorway.

Her dress was filthy from the dirty floor against which she had knelt and her face streamed with sweat. As she walked toward them the drums, which had never stopped beating, changed their tempo. Robert rose to meet her.

"They are playing the death dirge, Robert. I couldn't save her. I let her die. The old woman broke both her ankles so that she could never return to haunt them. I heard them snap."

They had both forgotten Marjorie. She lay and watched Robert take both of Charis' elbows in his hands. "Stop it, Charis! Stop it! We know that only God is the author and the end of life. We can only be used by Him. We are only His instruments. I know you did all you could."

He took his clean handkerchief from his pocket and gently wiped her sweaty face. The lantern flamed high for a second, and in that fraction of time Marjorie saw the expression on her husband's face as he looked at Charis, and she covered her own face with her hands.

Charis went back to the bungalow that night, but they felt it wiser for her to stay in the Christian home until morning. Robert slept on a mat by her side. But sleep eluded her. And through the long night hours she lay awake, and her own thoughts were more maddening to her than the steady beat of the drums.

CHAPTER 7

Marjorie spent the next week in bed. It gave her a prolonged period with nothing to do but think. After the initial shock had passed of discovering her husband's feeling for Charis, she was dominated by a sense of embarrassment. She wondered now if the cable she had so rashly sent to Robert had been as welcome as she had expected it to be. Had Robert felt the engagement had required of him the final step of marriage when she had thrown herself at his head?

Then like a pendulum her emotions had swung to the other extreme, and she became indignant. How dared he be disloyal to her in his heart? Never for a moment did Marjorie doubt his external compliance to the strict Christian marriage code, but it gave her little satisfaction to think it was his morals and not his heart that bound him to her.

If they had not been Christians there would now be no problem. She would divorce Robert and set him free. Or would she without putting up a fight? It would be the civilized thing to do. How odd that it would be the civilized yet not the Christian thing to do. How far marriage morals had departed from Biblical standards, that it would be considered the decent thing to do to divorce an erring husband in order to permit him to enjoy without social ostracism an adulterous situation forever.

What does he find in Charis that I lack? she thought petulantly. *She's an old maid. She looks like an old maid. She even acts like an old maid.* The question was answered in her mind by remembering Charis in the heathen hut with the dying woman. *Perhaps in India inner beauty, and the things of the spirit, loom more important than they do in the States. There are always many crises here revealing a person for what he really is.*

Robert and I are married for better or for worse. Our situation cannot change. Marjorie always returned to this unchangeable fact. *But perhaps I can. If I can grow up into a woman of character, maybe then Robert will love me again.* A wave of nausea swept over her. Oh, dear! It was going to be rather difficult to achieve these heights while going through the devastating pangs of morning sickness!

Robert, too, had a period of self-analysis. It had seemed to him advisable to sit down and calmly think through his unsought problem. In every situation, it seemed of late, in which he found himself the observer, his wife was not faring well by comparison to Charis. It was Charis always who played the leading role. She was not stealing the part from another player; it was just that the other player refused to perform at all.

Idly he drew three large circles, and divided them neatly into segments. He put no names above them, but in the circle which represented his own personality he put down characteristics common to him. It was an old classroom experiment. "Enjoys reading," he wrote first. "Enjoys athletics." "Serious minded," he placed in the third segment. "Quiet disposition." He crossed this through and wrote instead, "Stolid." "Takes work seriously." "Enjoys music." His orbit was full.

He turned to the second circle which represented Marjorie. "Pretty," he wrote in the first segment. "Athletic," he added. He compared the circle with his own. Enjoys reading? Had Marjorie to his knowledge ever read a book after her college days? Serious minded? Marjorie was always flippant. Quiet? Stolid? Hardly. Marjorie was quicksilver and quiet of any sort bored her. Work interests? Certainly there was no dovetailing there. Music? Not the type he enjoyed. He left the rest of the circle blank.

Happiness in marriage, one professor had said, occurred at its best when these circles complemented each other perfectly. Other than a physical attraction and a shared interest in some sports, actually what did Marjorie and he have in common? And yet surely he would not have married her without some deeper attraction.

As he turned to the last circle he realized why he found Charis so attractive. Their personalities, he could see at a glance, could reach out on every plane and find completion in the other. There were no ragged ends, no blank segments. Still, in all honesty he wondered if he had seen Charis and Marjorie on the same college campus, would he not have made the same

SONG BY THE RIVER

decision? He could not blame his tragedy on the timing of his meeting with each woman. Even if he had known Charis first, would he have been able to escape the gamin appeal of Marjorie? Only the backward look showed him what could have been, perhaps what should have been.

Knowing these facts, and facing them, could he still salvage his own marriage? Happiness for a Christian could only be found in the marriage bond, of this he was convinced. Was there any possibility of finding any in the shambles of his own? Could he stop this corrosion which was eating at them both? There was a new life to consider now.

"God, please help us," he prayed.

A determined effort to try to better things found Robert suggesting to Marjorie that she might enjoy learning to shoot. They erected a rifle range back of the bungalow for their use. Every year they had several hunts in the jungle mainly to entertain guests, but partly to secure meat to make possible a change from the scrawny chicken and strong goat meat that was their normal diet. These hunts were a colorful and carefully arranged event, and Robert knew that they would afford entertainment for Marjorie.

His wife was an apt pupil. Their time together on the range was unstrained and pleasant, but in spite of all his good intentions, Robert's work at the hospital encroached more and more on his free time, and finally Marjorie was also left by herself with this pastime. She kept at it faithfully for a while, so much so that it sounded as if the mission compound must be engaging in an all-out war. The bombardment of shots could be heard clearly even from the hospital. Robert did not think it was a bad idea for the village to be informed that the Memsahib-ji was a good shot. This constant talk about *Swa-raj* made him feel an undercurrent of worry about the possibility of danger to the women at his station when it arrived. Like many others, although he was in favor of an independent nation, he feared its birth pangs.

It was the Babu, finally, who found a genuine outlet for Marjorie's abundant energy, which, even as her pregnancy advanced, did not abate. He had been pleased with her progress in Hindii, and suggested that the Rajah of Surrak Annund was seeking an English teacher to instruct his wife. Custom prohibited him, a man, from penetrating behind the strict *purdah* that the Rajah's wife observed. But he had suggested that his star pupil, the new Memsahib-ji, might be interested. The Rajah had indicated his approval of the plan.

Marjorie was excited by the opportunity. She had never been inside the palace. Robert was glad to have his wife kept busy in this way. It was a white-collared, refined type of missionary service just made to order for her. He only hoped it would hold her quicksilver interest.

As Marjorie walked through the crowded village streets on her first trip to the palace she was as usual followed by a crowd of curious people. The little naked children cluttered her path, salaaming her. Their eyes were sore and runny, attracting the ever present flies. The children were so accustomed to them that they did not even bother to flick them away, and their eyelashes were beaded with them. She knew that if Charis were here she would stop and hug even the dirtiest of them. "Ugh!"

At Babu-ji's side she picked her way daintily around the sewage which was merely dumped out the front door, where scavenger dogs pounced upon it. Then suddenly the narrow winding mud road widened and there against this squalor was the palace in all its beauty. It rose like a lotus from the mud. It was all that she had imagined a palace should be in her fairy tale days.

The steps were wide and circular. The veranda railing was of latticed marble. The marble walls were decorated to eye level with exquisite pictures of flowers wrought by inlaid precious stones and mother of pearl.

The Rajah, dressed in European clothes, was standing at the top of the stairs to greet them. He shook hands and took them to some rattan chairs which had been placed by the railing which overlooked the river. A strong fragrance of jasmine and champa blossoms from the palace garden reached them there.

The Rajah was short and swarthy. He had intelligent shrewd black eyes. It was, however, the benign expression on his face that gave it its predominant characteristic. He was a good ruler, Marjorie had heard, and seeing him she believed it.

"Perhaps you are surprised that I desire that my wife learn English." He spoke with a clipped Oxford accent. He did not wait for a reply. "I am somewhat modern in my ideas. I want my wife to be educated. I want her to meet a woman who is intelligent, who can teach her English, and also give her some companionship other than that of the giggly harem women. She is, I must tell you, rather reluctant and shy at this break from tradition I am proposing. But she is doing it to please me. She has been taught that a woman's knowledge should not extend beyond the oven. Our lawgiver, Manu, our Indian Moses, has written that in his code. But the *Puranas*, another holy book, teaches that, 'A woman who wishes to perform sacred oblations should wash the feet of her Lord and drink the water, for the husband is to the wife greater than the God Siva. He is her Lord, her priest and her religion. Wherefore forsaking all else, she ought chiefly to worship her husband.'

"I have dispensed with the footwashing in my marital demands; but I am insisting on this English study, and Sundri is obedient to my commands. It is fortunate that you are so beautiful." He spoke of her as if appraising a piece of jewelry. Hindu men, Marjorie had discovered, were able to maintain a surprising objectivity.

"Do you have any questions?" the Rajah asked.

"Only one. Do you object to my teaching your wife to read from our English Bible?"

"And if I did?"

"The mission would not feel that I was justified in the time it would take just to teach your wife to read."

"Are you warning me that you will try to make a Christian of my wife?" His eyes twinkled at her.

Marjorie studied her answer before giving it gravely, "Yes, I am."

"You have my permission." He smiled. "You will find it hard to convert a Hindu. Our religion is already all-inclusive. We are like a giant octopus; we simply absorb a new faith and it becomes a part of our own. Our women are especially hard to reach for they are tenacious in their religious beliefs. You would have better success with me. I have read your Bible and I have found much in it that speaks to my heart."

As he spoke he rose to his feet and walked to the door of the palace. He clapped his hands imperiously. A white-turbaned servant prostrated himself at his feet and unlaced his shoes. With dignity, in his stockinged feet, the Rajah preceded her into the palace. At Babu-ji's direction Marjorie slipped out of her softshoed moccasins and followed the Rajah as he led her through an exquisite room, across thick Oriental rugs. The softness felt through her thin nylons was a sensuous impression she always retained of this fairy place.

After going through seemingly endless corridors they reached still another door. "This," he said, "is the court for the women. I have only one wife. I am allowed as many as I wish. But in this I think your religion is right. A man does not find in numbers a joy which he can find in one. You will understand, I know, my feelings when you meet the Rani. I shall leave you here. She wants to meet you alone."

He clapped his hands again and the door swung open from within. Marjorie found herself in a dark room, almost completely devoid of sunlight. As her eyes adjusted themselves to the change in light she noticed that one whole wall of the room was an exquisite marble screen. As she looked at it she caught the flutter of a sari through the holes. She looked away, but she was still conscious of the eyes upon her.

In one corner of the room was a phonograph. It was an old-fashioned Edison, and looked incongruous in its place of honor. The whole room was filled with a number of strange things. It did not show the taste which she had noticed in the outer rooms.

She heard the tinkle of bracelets before she saw Sundri, Rani of Surrak Annund. Nothing had prepared her for the beautiful girl who stepped through the doorway. She was just a girl, not more than fourteen, Marjorie guessed. Her sari was the palest pink, and where the border fell about her waist it was richly embroidered with pure spun gold. Her eyes were almost oblong. Outlined as they were by dark kohl, it gave her tiny face the look of being all eyes. She was *Shahrazad*, all the fairy princesses of all time.

The Rani came toward her, and both women touched their foreheads in a salaam. Then they sat down together on a divan which was raised slightly from the floor and piled deep with cushions. Marjorie gave her short prepared speech in Hindii and started with the English lesson.

Pointing to various objects in the room, she enunciated distinctly their English names. Like a little parrot the Rani repeated the words after her. Like a child with a new toy, she was delighted with the game. When Marjorie pointed to the phonograph, the Rani went over and turning the crank, played a record that was obviously in her honor. Frank Sinatra's inti-

SONG BY THE RIVER

mate voice whispered out at them. They both laughed together. Time went by and still the Rani did not ask her guest to leave. She seemed loath to let her go. Babu-ji, who had been coaching Marjori on court etiquette, had made it clear to her that she was not to leave until her hostess dismissed her. Finally, in desperation, Marjorie looked at her watch, and sadly the little regent took the broad hint.

"Thank you," she said in English, "now you may go." It was a rehearsed sentence, and Marjorie smiled at the reluctance with which it was said.

And so began Marjorie's tutorship of the Rani of Surrak Annund. She went to the palace once a week. In time she wondered which one enjoyed the contact most, the Rani who saw in her an unknown world, or herself who felt welcome and needed for the first time since she had come to India.

CHAPTER 8

EVERY MORNING IT WAS the Muezzin's call to prayer that awakened the village of Surrak Annund. Mohammed, it was said, had sought a medium for announcing the call to Allah other than the trumpet which played such an important role in Judaism or the bells which were more peculiarly Christian. In the end he had selected the effective musical instrument of the human voice. Anyone who lived within the voice range of the mosque could not fail to hear the penetrating intoning of the Muezzin of the ninety and nine names for Allah.

But on Sunday morning the ringing of the church bells in Surrak Annund competed with the Muezzin's voice and reminded the villagers of the church of God in their midst. Many heard and answered the summons. They came from the village itself and also from various nearby Christian settlements. They all came dressed to the glory of God. In some cases these Sunday bests were none too good, but at least all worshipers came washed and scrubbed.

The little children wore the dresses which came from the States. Every Christmas each child received a dress and a toy. These were carefully rolled up in newspaper and distributed on this gala day. The dress was to last for the year. Since few boy's pants and shirts were sent to the mission, boys and girls dressed indiscriminately alike in dresses. Many wore them inside out. For when any dress became dirty it was considered a waste not to wear the other side before it was washed. No matter how the part of clothing looked which was closest to a little brown body, at least the part that showed was clean.

Although the outside of the church of Surrak Annund was European in architecture and followed the traditional style of the nave on the inside, in all other ways it accommodated itself to the Orient. Instead of pews, matting was spread on both sides of the aisle. Men customarily sat on the right, and the women on the left. The women, still close to the customs which centuries of Hinduism had forced upon them, hesitated to sit in front of their husbands. They compromised by sitting out of sight across the aisle. The Code of Manu, under which most of them had been reared, taught them that a man must not look at his wife while she sits, eats, sneezes or yawns.

As the women squatted cross-legged on the mats, one could see the wisdom of the Indian seer's advice. Truly there are more attractive moments in a woman's life.

Marjorie usually sat between Charis and Anugra. The two white women tucked their legs both on the same side. But all the others folded one foot under the knee of the other — except the mothers. They had a practical sitting posture of their own. They usually stretched their legs straight out in front of them. The infants were placed with their little brown heads resting against their mothers' feet. When they became restless the mothers moved their legs up and down, and the soothing, rocking motion proved its frequent success by the sleeping babies. If this failed to quiet the child, with no embarrassment to anyone the mothers would suckle the babies under a fold of the flowing sari, and the service would continue with no further interruption.

Charis loved the church service. The Indian *bhuguns* with their accompaniment by the church musician, often just a drummer, but sometimes aided by a native flutist, always flooded her heart with memories of her father who had transcribed many of these native songs into their permanent form.

Robert, sitting cross-legged across from them in the men's section, always towered head and shoulders above them all. Most of the Hindu men had short legs and also short bodies. Robert was both long limbed and long torsoed. Even sitting, he was tall. His sandy hair, which verged on red, was kept short, but where it had a chance it tended to curl. His features, unlike those of the natives, were thin. His face was long, the typical English horseface, the Indians called it. His eyes were the most noticed part of his face. It was not so much the shape or the color but the way they reflected his thoughts. They were talking eyes. But what made him attractive was his smile. When in repose his face verged on the dour. But when he smiled few failed to smile with him. He had the gift of laughter, especially the rare gift of being able to laugh at himself.

Although he looked so different from the men about him, one could tell he felt one with them in spirit, as he joined in the worship service with them. His nasal American enunciation of the Hindii words could be heard above the softer singing of the natives. He did not speak like a native; but what was more important, he felt like one of them.

Marjorie spent most of the time while the others sang trying to decipher the words in the Sanskrit alphabet. It was tedious for her to go to church when she understood next to nothing. But Robert was insistent that a Christian's place on Sunday morning — barring illness — was in the place of God. It was a sin to absent oneself from divine worship. And so she sat uncomfortable and unhappy on the floor matting and endured the service.

Pastor Biswas never raised his voice. Although Marjorie did not understand the words, it seemed to her he never became excited over his message. But those who understood him appreciated the effortless delivery. Robert was especially aware of the man's keen mind, and above all, the way in which he was able to bring transcendental thoughts to the ordinary plane on which his flock moved. They were being well fed.

Anugra was especially warmed by the messages. The pastor was her foster brother, and she knew from long experience that he was also a living epistle. The deeply religious home life which she was able to share with him and his wife was a constant source of blessing to her. It was good, too, that he had been given the gift of prophecy, of interpretation.

Her brother had chosen as his morning text the third commandment, "Thou shalt not take the name of the Lord thy God in vain." It was not necessary for Pastor Biswas to labor the obvious meaning of the commandment. For no Hindu woman would dare take even her husband's name in vain. In fact the women would not, even after conversion, refer to their husbands by name. They would speak of them as "the father of my children" or identify them by the trade they practiced or in some other polite indirect way. Even Pastor Biswas' own wife had her awkward moments when she taught her Sunday school class of women. Whenever a Bible text she was required to read contained the word Biswas or faith — and many did — she

SONG BY THE RIVER 41

was constrained to avoid the word. She would pause deliberately and let her well-trained hearers delicately fill in for themselves the missing word.

The pastor spent his time this morning developing the way in which we break the commandment in prayer. He illustrated his point by reminding the people how often they prayed the Lord's Prayer with no thoughtful application. It became too often merely a vain repetition, like that of the ninety and nine names for Allah which they heard on every hand. He pointed out how the record of the Lord's Prayer in Matthew followed immediately after the warning about the use of vain repetitions. "We can be irreverent even in our act of prayer. We can sin even while in the act of divine worship." As he concluded with these words he challenged his congregation to pray this morning with him the Lord's Prayer.

It was a simple message, but its effectiveness could be seen by the fervent recitation of the prayer by the worshipers. Even the tiniest voices joined with feeling in the familiar words, "Hallowed be Thy name . . ."

There is no church anywhere on earth, Robert thought with appreciation, *where this morning God's name has been hallowed more earnestly and more effectively than here in the church of Surrak Annund.* And he was grateful to be able to be one of the flock of his friend, Pastor Biswas.

CHAPTER 9

"AK CHEMISE, DO CHEMISE, TEEN CHEMISE . . . ." The *dhobi* sat cross-legged on the floor of the Townsend annex room. Marjorie sat at her dressing table with pencil poised in her hand until the count on shirts was finished.

This counting of wash clothes was a routine of Monday and Thursday mornings. At first Marjorie had protested with Robert about the necessity for counting the laundry; but when she had neglected to do so one Monday and the wash that returned that Thursday had been lacking in some of her choicest linens, she realized the wisdom of the count.

Ethics on stealing were quite obviously "steal if steal can." There was no feeling of guilt even among most Christians unless the culprit was caught redhanded. Clothing had to be counted before being given to the washerman. Food and flour and sugar — all must be carefully measured before being handed out to the cook. In non-Christian circles the cook assumed that a certain amount of petty thievery was his due, a part of his salary. But Robert was strict that none of this be allowed or encouraged by a sloppy housekeeping on Marjorie's part. Dhunwa should be paid enough that he would feel that his salary was adequate, and he was informed and reminded by daily checks that he need not supplement his wages in an underhanded way.

When dealing with the heathen, one would assume the ethics in which they had been reared. But it was most discouraging to have to fight for the existence of the eighth commandment within the church group. The church at Surrak Annund would be most uneasy when Pastor Biswas in his series reached this particular commandment, for stealing seemed to be a deeply ingrained sin and an almost universal one.

So Marjorie watched carefully that the *dhobi* would not be able to smuggle an extra shirt into his bag. When the final count, *dus chemise*, had been given, she recorded faithfully in her book, "Ten shirts." *Dhobi* respected the figures she wrote. "It is written," carried great weight in any subsequent arguments.

The laundry count was time consuming. Perhaps it helped the *dhobi's* morals. But it was always an irritation for Marjorie, especially when the laundry was counted on its return. It would now return intact in number, but too often the more delicate fabrics would come back in rags. The pounding on the rocks in lieu of laundry soap, and the long drying and bleaching in the hot sun were not what the manufacturers had anticipated. It was no wonder missionaries came out with trunkloads of essential clothing.

At first the idea of a retinue of servants had been appealing to Marjorie. But now that she had to manage them she longed for the easier American way of the machine supplanting human labor.

Robert had explained to her that many of those who served about the compound did so out of economic necessity. Their acceptance of Christ had made outcastes of them and cut them off from their regular channels of work. Some few Christians were able to continue in the work in which their birth by caste had placed them. This was always encouraged when it was possible. But these few could be counted on one hand. Mission opinion was always divided about what to do with these unemployed Christians. Rather than dole out food on a charity basis, Robert preferred to make jobs if necessary for these Christian outcastes about the mission compound.

Tilak, the water carrier, would not any longer be able to carry his water to the Hindus. He was now a Christian, and the water from his goatskin bag would be defiling. And so he had become the mission water carrier. It was his task to carry the water from the well to the house where it was stored in empty petrol tins. Since this was scarcely enough work to keep him busy, the garden had been assigned also to him. He had green fingers, and in season the mission enjoyed delicious bananas, oranges, lentils and beans. Even tomatoes had been introduced and prospered under his hands.

The *chowkidar*, (night watchman), had formerly been in the employ of a wealthy merchant in the village. Now his presence in the home, his very shadow, could defile the household of the high caste merchant of the Vaisya caste. It was the custom of thieves to respect the presence of a watchman — even one as negligible as Sanjhu. And he had been added to the list of household employees.

Soon there would have to be an *ayah*, a woman whose job it would be during the day to carefully watch over the new baby. Hazards to infancy and childhood were doubled by the Indian environment. The *ayah* would be the all-seeing eye which kept the baby from picking up a scorpion. She would check the baby's tiny shoes to see that no deadly insect had crawled into them for comfort during the damp rains. She would shake the bedding of the baby's bed to be sure a cobra had not decided to curl to sleep under the ruffled spread.

Now the only woman employed was for cleaning purposes. She had been a Chumar of the sweeper caste, and had been well-trained in her caste work. Once Marjorie made the mistake of asking Dhunwa to sweep the kitchen floor. He had been deeply insulted. The dignity of common toil, the Christian principle, was so foreign to the converts that for the most part the mission did not force these babes in Christ into jobs which went against the grain, the grain of the caste to which they no longer belonged, but in which their traditional roots lay.

The woman's husband helped her in the heavier work which fell to the sweeper caste — since there was no septic tank system as yet in the mission bungalow. It would also be this man who would wash the baby's diapers if Marjorie cared to delegate the job to another. Men usually washed all clothes, even baby clothes. But the usual *dhobi* would be forbidden by caste to touch diapers. Thus the division of labor divided and subdivided itself.

Dhunwa, the cook, combined the jobs of serving, cooking and washing the dishes. He was breaking tradition to do so. Usually three different people of three different castes would have been required.

Mohardas, the *punkha* boy, was from a village back in the jungles across the river. His job made it possible for him to board with a Christian family living in Surrak Annund and attend the mission school. His father, although a Christian, because of his great skill with animals and because of the religious tolerance of the Rajah of Surrak Annund, had been one of the few Christians to keep his job. He was chief elephant caretaker of the palace. His wife, however, preferred to remain in their home village.

Of this group employed on the mission compound, only the man and wife who served as sweepers could have kept their village jobs. Since on the other hand it was difficult to get Christians, converts from higher castes, to volunteer for this menial work, the Christian sweeper and his wife had been hired also by the mission.

Recently in the large city of Nagpur the sweepers, the latrine cleaners, had gone on strike. Pandit Shudla, an orthodox Brahmin, when things became too bad to endure, issued an appeal to all citizens to do their own cleaning, and set the example himself. People, instead of supporting his civic attitude, deplored it indignantly. Strangely enough, the most aggressive opponents of the Pandit were the sweepers themselves, who were outraged at this unfair method — they claimed — of strike breaking. Caste and its strict boundary lines of limitations were strange indeed, and a problem even in the indigenous church.

On Marjorie's account book the salaries of these workers were as follows:

Monthly wage

Cook	20 Rupees	Approximately	$5.00
Gardener	16 Rupees	Approximately	$4.00
Watchman	12 Rupees	Approximately	$3.00
Washerman	12 Rupees	Approximately	$3.00
Sweepers	8 Rupees	Approximately	$2.00
Punkha boy	4 Rupees	Approximately	$1.00
Total Expenditure	72 Rupees	Approximately	$18.00

Enough rice to feed the average family ran about two annas or about five cents a day. Since homes were supplied rent free for all the workers, the mission staff by comparison with the village workers were well paid.

Whatever privacy one might otherwise have managed was made completely impossible when one was surrounded by this wall of eyes. Even the privacy of the bathroom could be invaded by the delicate coughing of the sweeper to make sure it was a convenient time for his visit.

A veteran lady missionary, Dr. Glendenning of Burrapur, their closest mission station, had told Marjorie of a rumor about herself that had been started and rolled along until it finally reached even her ears. It seemed the good doctor had brought with her a record of calisthenics from the States and had endured every morning much needed sitting-up exercises to music in what she erroneously thought was the privacy of her own bedroom. It was reported to her, finally, that the good lady was seen to do *puja* (worship), to a little god who sang to her from a box. No doubt her observers had been hard put to find any other explanation for her calisthenics. After that, phonograph and record had gathered dust, and it was quite obvious that Dr. Glendenning had settled down to a life of accumulating avoirdupois.

Unquestionably Marjorie would gladly trade all of her retinue for an automatic washing machine, an electric range, an electric sweeper and—blissful thought—a bathroom with modern plumbing.

CHAPTER 10

THERE WERE TWO CASES in the hospital which Charis felt concerned about in a special way. They were for her more than just professional patients, and she felt a certain self identification with each of them.

The first of these was the pathetic Putkin. This poor village woman had been led astray from the strict path of virtue, and her husband had taken his lawful right and slashed away her nose.

Charis had been enraged and horrified when the poor woman had come screaming into the hospital, her face a mass of mutilated flesh. She had known Putkin since she had been a small child. She was the daughter of the village sweet seller. Often she had seen the little girl hovering by her father's elbow as he dropped the delicious fat jellabees into the hot *ghee*, and dipped them into their sugar coating while still warm. Whenever she had gone to the bazaar with her father she had begged to pass the sweet seller's stall; and many a jellabee had found its way — warm and sticky — into her own little hand, a present for the *chotibaba* from the kind man.

Although Putkin's father had never become a Christian, he had been an admirer of her father, and the two girls so similar in age had carried on a shy friendship until as was the custom little Putkin had been betrothed at the age of eight, and her marriage consummated when she was twelve. Her husband, a wealthy merchant of the village, even then had nothing but his gold to commend him.

Charis could scarcely bear to look at the poor woman's face. Yet in a way Putkin was fortunate. For Robert was already talking of the possibility of sending her to Lahore to a fine surgeon who had come to the country and who specialized in plastic surgery. And since Putkin's husband had cast her off

47

and marked her for life as an unfaithful woman, she was dead to him, and the mission was free to do with the discard what they wished.

And Putkin, the patient, had turned eagerly to the faithful Bible women who visited the women's ward daily. She had learned from them, to her amazement, that God was more forgiving than her husband, and that her repentant heart could find forgiveness and solace in the church He had ordained on earth. Life for her was beginning again.

The other patient to whom Charis was drawn in a special way was a small twelve-year-old girl, Elizabeth, the daughter of a Christian who lived back in the jungles. She was sweet, quick to learn, and Charis knew, also dreadfully ill. She examined her chart with an aching heart each day. The prognosis was always negative.

This morning Charis' heart fell as Anugra met her at the door of the hospital.

"Elizabeth is asking for you," the nurse informed her.

Charis went directly to the small private room in which the young girl had been placed. The child's breathing was labored, and as Charis put her hands on her forehead, without even looking at the chart she knew the high fever had returned during the night. Elizabeth turned her face as she felt the cool hand. But she did not speak. Only her eyes attempted speech, and Charis knew that she was recognized.

"Your father is coming to visit you today." Charis was glad to be able to give this news. She had sent a letter back into the village where the child's father lived, and seeing her condition she only hoped the man would arrive in time.

The cracked lips rallied with a smile. Charis sat quietly by her little patient. The child complained little, and for a time they had had high hopes that she would recover; but her case of tuberculosis had been too advanced to yield to healing. This comparatively new disease seemed especially fatal to the Indians. It was perhaps because they had not had generations of time to build up an immunity to it, and while they recovered from many diseases which would wreak havoc on a European, on the other hand, the hospital had not been successful with its more advanced tubercular patients.

Charis dreaded to break the news to Golab, the child's only living relative. The poor man had already lost his wife and two other children from the disease. He had been a first generation Christian, converted by her father in one of the evangelistic tours he took back into the jungles twice a year. He had had little chance for much deeper Bible training, for he himself was the only witness to the Truth in the little village in which he continued to live. But he had learned to read, and was faithful in his slow efforts to read the Scriptures. Elizabeth had been born about the time he had started reading through the Gospel of John, and he and his wife had selected the Christian name.

The villagers had been taunting him because ever since his conversion one sorrow after another had come upon him. The man had been magnificent, a second Job, through all this suffering. But Charis shrank back from having to break this further climactic piece of sad news, and feared for the effect it could have on his spiritual life. She prayed for wisdom, to be guided to the right words to say; even while she prayed she felt a hand on her shoulder. It was Anugra. "Golab is outside."

Charis pressed the child's hand. "Your father has come. I will bring him in." Elizabeth was still conscious. Charis found the father waiting in the corridor. There was no expression on his face. In the end she did not need to speak. Seeing the anguish in her own eyes he asked simply, "How long does she have to live?"

"She may live until the morning."

"May I go in to her?"

Mutely, Charis led the way. When the man walked on his bare feet soundlessly over the cement floor to the child's bedside she left the door slightly ajar, and stood, a silent listener to the conversation.

"Elizabeth! Elizabeth!" His voice called to his daughter as if she had already gone to another country.

But the child responded. "Dudda!" She used the child's form of endearment.

"They tell me, Pyari, my beloved, that by tomorrow you will be with Jesus. Can you still hear me?"

She must have nodded, for with no lack of control evident, his strong tender voice continued, "When you get to heaven, I want you to do something for me."

"I will do whatever you ask, Dudda." The voice was surprisingly strong.

"My darling, seek out the Christ; and when you have found Him, fall down at His feet and kiss them for me."

Charis felt her eyes spill over with tears, and not wanting to have her lack of control seen by anyone, she stumbled blindly into an adjacent room which was empty.

What a parting message to give to a loved one. Such faith from a first generation Christian, and one who has been almost completely self tutored in the Scriptures. And here am I, Charis thought, *who have had every advantage, and my own faith and trust are weak. Every day, every week, these babes in Christ put me to shame.*

"O God in heaven," she prayed in desperation, "while Elizabeth seeks Thee out in Glory, grant that I may truly learn to kiss Thy feet here on earth. In Jesus' name I pray, Amen."

CHAPTER 11

CHARIS ANTICIPATED HIS EVERY MOVE in the operation. It was scarcely ever necessary for Robert to define specifically the instrument needed. It was always placed in his hand. As he finished suturing up the incision he looked across the table at his efficient helper.

Her nurse's uniform was flattering to Charis. Often, while an intern, Robert had been surprised at how he had failed to recognize the nurses with whom he made the hospital rounds when they were off duty and dressed in street clothes. Most of them were improved in appearance when dressed in the more feminine styles. But there was a severity about the uniform which enhanced the simplicity of beauty which Charis possessed. Her very good features were framed nun-like by the nurse's cap; and even the practical shoes which she always wore did not look so heavy and clumsy under the starched white skirt.

As Anugra wheeled the patient out of the operating room he turned to Charis. "Wait, a moment, I must talk to you."

She stood ill at ease while he removed his doctor's gown and rubber gloves and scrubbed his hands.

"When are you going on your vacation?" he asked.

"Whenever it will best dovetail with yours. One of us should stay here, don't you think?"

"I have been selfish not to speak of our plans sooner. We are not going to the hills this summer. I do not want to risk the long train trip with Marjorie. So plan your trip as soon as you wish. Do you have anyone to go with?" He asked as an afterthought.

"Miss Clarence asked me to go with her if I could arrange it."

Robert grimaced. "Is there no one else?"

Charis flushed. "I have known Miss Clarence all my life."

"That still does not make her the ideal traveling companion. You need a rest, a complete change. If you take this trip with that hypochondriac you may as well stay here and administer pills. What about Dr. Glendenning? She is always a refreshing breeze."

Charis' face lightened. "If I could only go with her, but she is not free to leave the hospital right now. I did ask her."

"What you really need is to get away from us all. If it were not for the unsettled condition of the railroads, the strikes that are endangering travel, the untraceable derailments, I would urge you to go by yourself."

"If you don't mind, Robert, I would rather let the matter go temporarily."

"I do mind, Charis. You're too good a nurse for me to enjoy seeing you . . . ." He stopped in the middle of his sentence.

Her wide eyes challenged him. "Finish what you were going to say, Robert."

"All right, Charis. I will. You are going the same route Miss Clarence took."

"No. Oh, no!"

"I shouldn't have spoken. I sometimes wonder, Charis, if you are impersonal enough to be a good nurse. When Elizabeth died, it was not just another patient; it was as if you had lost your own child. You can't take to your heart all the suffering you see about you and not crack under the strain. You must . . . ."

"You are wrong, Robert. I know my trouble has nothing to do with my hospital work."

"Then what is it, Charis?" He looked directly at her, and as he looked he saw for one moment a look of anguish which was almost immediately extinguished. But he had seen enough.

"Is it working with me, Charis? Am I too demanding?"

But even as he asked the question he knew that he had misread her eyes. It was as well that he had. She bared her heart with a look, then excused herself and left the room.

Robert walked slowly to the wide window of the operating room. There was no longer any doubt in his mind that Charis Brown was in love with him. It was an intolerable situation. Something must be done. No words had passed between them, but they had not been needed. A woman as highly sensitive as he knew Charis to be must have read his admiration a hundred times a day in his eyes.

He pounded the desk. Perhaps Doctor Glendenning could arrange a transfer. Maybe she could be persuaded to request that Charis be transferred to the Burrapur Hospital. This situation could not be permitted to continue a day longer than necessary.

For him there was this constant struggle with his emotions, his feeling of guilt even when he managed to sublimate his feelings. But what was worse, now it seemed certain that Charis too was being harmed by their geographical prison. He was afraid that she — if help did not come in time — would be driven by her conflicting loyalties and stern religious principles to walk over the precipice into the blank abyss of madness.

The doctor in him, as well as the man, having diagnosed the situation, was determined to remedy it. "I shall speak to Glendenning on my next trip into Burrapur," he decided. Satisfied in a measure that he had at last decided on some definite action, he settled down to resume the ordinary medical duties that fortunately kept him from any further thought.

Charis, in her naivete, fortunately did not realize how transparent she had been. Her hidden feelings, which she had kept suppressed so long even from herself, had so horrified her as she had for the first time really caught an intimation of them that she had resorted to flight, flight into the tremendous activity of the day's duties. And so in their work both Robert and Charis found an anesthetic which postponed the results of the revelation of the day.

CHAPTER 12

"CHARIS, WHAT DID YOU DO with your evenings when you were a young girl?"

Charis smiled across the table at Marjorie. "My father and I would often read aloud to each other. But perhaps our favorite pastime was our musical evenings. My father was especially interested in the native oriental music and has set a great many of our religious hymn lyrics to oriental tunes."

"Charis herself," interrupted Robert, "plays many oriental instruments. She is especially proficient with the lute. Why not play for us after dinner? I haven't heard you play and sing for a long time."

While Dhunwa cleared the table, they carried a lamp through the archway and set it on the piano. The living room glowed with its amber light. This was the only room in which they had a rug. It belonged to Charis, and was a lovely Bokhara which her father had given to her mother when they had first come to India. It had only become more beautiful with age. The lamp glow kindled its saffron tones. It was pleasant to Marjorie to sink down on the cool rattan couch. Robert sprawled in his favorite fan-backed chair. Charis with native grace dropped to the floor, and, crossing her legs like an Indian, began to pluck a few strings on her lute. "Any favorites?" She asked.

"Kashmiri Love Song." It was the only oriental melody Marjorie knew. With her throaty deep contralto that blended so well with the lute, Charis complied. "Pale hands I loved beside the Shalimar . . . ."

"Sing something of Rabindranath Tagore," Robert requested next. "The voice of wayside pansies, that do not attract the careless glance murmurs in these desultory lines . . . ," he quoted from the poet.

She sang one in Bengali. "Will you translate it for us

SONG BY THE RIVER

please, Charis? Bengali is too different from the Hindii for me to understand," Robert asked.

Charis fumbled with the words,

> If you would have it so, I will end my singing . . . .
> If it suddenly startles you in your walk, I will step aside and take another path . . . .
> If it confuses you in your flower-weaving, I will shun your lonely garden.
> If it makes the water wanton and wild, I will not row my boat by your bank.

Then she sang it again in Bengali. And as she sang, Robert hummed an accompaniment, a promise, "I will not row my boat by your bank."

"Now it is your turn," Marjorie broke the spell. "Sing us your favorite one, Charis."

"I am fond of Sarojini Naidu's lyrics, especially her songs of life and death taken from her collection *The Sceptred Flute*. 'Why should a song-bird like you have a broken wing?' They have a decadent flavor, but they appeal to me." She strummed on her lute and then started to sing "The Offering."

> Were beauty mine, Beloved, I would bring it
> Like a rare blossom to Love's glowing shrine;
> Were dear youth mine, Beloved, I would fling it
> Like a rich pearl into Love's lustrous wine . . . .
> But I have naught save my heart's deathless passion
> That craves no recompense divinely sweet,
> Content to wait in proud and lowly fashion,
> And kiss the shadow of Love's passing feet.

Is she in love with Robert because he is Robert? thought Marjorie. *Or is it just his blatant masculinity that appeals to her? It probably helps that he is the only white male within a radius of one hundred miles.* She looked over at her tall lanky husband. *Robert should be locked up. He has entirely too much charm to be loose in this female jungle.*

"I had not realized," her husband was saying, "that India's outstanding statesman was also so good a poet and so much a woman."

"Her new busy schedule will now no doubt crowd out any further writing!" Charis started to put away her lute.

"Wait! Before you stop, Charis, sing us some *bhuguns*, please."

The night became filled with the music of the Indian native hymns. As always happened, out on the veranda the *chowkidar* heard and joined in. Dhunwa heard him and added his voice from the kitchen. The *punkha walla* listened then joined in the refrain. Soon others heard and a chorus of voices from the darkness sang the sad words, "*Oh mara jan akala hai . . . .*"

Robert went and sat beside Marjorie on the couch, and as the Hindii was being sung he translated softly for her, "My soul was lonely. My soul was lonely. It did not know where to go. It did not know where to go. The Lord came and took me home."

"How strange," Robert said, "to find Augustine's cry of the human heart put to music in a strange land, 'My soul is restless until it finds its rest in Thee.'"

"And who was Augustine?" Marjorie asked. It was with this question that the musical evening ended.

Marjorie had been waking at the approach of dawn for several days now. She did not like this eerie time of morning, and was glad when the patches of light melted together to form the first uniform light of day. The "dappled dawn," Milton had called it. This morning she heard Robert stirring in the dressing room where he had been sleeping for the past month.

"Robert," she called.

He was already dressed to leave. "I thought I'd run over to the hospital early this morning. There are some cases which are critical. They need my attention."

"I do, too, Robert," she said plaintively.

"Marjorie," he smiled at her from the doorway, "you are a fine healthy specimen, and you are having a normal pregnancy. What more could you want?"

"I want to go home. I want my baby to be born in America. You have been here five years now. Couldn't we get leave?"

The smile left Robert's face. "Your condition, Marjorie, doesn't warrant the trip. In a normal birth, you know a doctor does little but stand by. A Hindu doctor once accused that we Americans had been able to make a racket out of obstetrics because of our pampered women. While I disagreed vehemently with him, still in most normal cases even I must admit a doctor is not necessary. There is no reason at all why we can't take care of you in our Surrak Annund Hospital. I shall arrange for Doctor Glendenning to come down if you would prefer to have her."

"I want to go home," she repeated.

"Marjorie! There is one thing that must be said and settled between us now. I don't intend to leave my work in India — ever. And I don't intend to humor you and take you home now. The sooner you realize that I mean this, and stop this everlasting effort to uproot me, the happier you will be. When you married me you married this country. It, too, is yours for better or for worse."

"And the baby will make no difference?"

"None at all."

"I am sorry that I ever joined you here."

"On that at least we agree."

Marjorie flushed and fell silent. Robert, thinking the conversation ended, turned to leave the room.

"Robert!"

He turned. "I'm sorry I said what I did. I did not mean it." Her voice was low.

He came back to the bed and took her hand in his. "I am sure that after the child comes it will make this seem more home to you. I know I am failing you." But even as he spoke gently, reassuringly to her, she could not help but notice that he did not retract his statement.

CHAPTER 13

ROBERT DID NOT KEEP his worries for very long in the hospital. There was too much here that demanded all his attention, and Marjorie was soon crowded out in the crises of the fight for life in which he found himself engaged. It seemed to him, sometimes, that all his cases were critical ones. He had no insured patients who came to convalesce from minor ailments to get something back from their investments. Here they came only when someone else carried them in.

Death was a familiar face in the hospital. It was never a stranger in India. He had read that in the Bengal famine one and a half million people had died. Yet the population had increased by four million that very year.

He broke his back trying to save the few that reached him to increase the already staggering number who swelled the population of this overcrowded land. There was never a time when he felt his work day over. He had read somewhere that if every doctor in India were multiplied by ten there would still only be one doctor to a thousand. There were only about two hundred and ninety hospitals with a capacity of about sixteen thousand beds in the entire country. Yet India had — take leprosy alone — a million lepers. And it had been estimated that to do a thorough clean up job it would be necessary to quarantine three hundred million people.

All he could do was help those who reached him. This he did conscientiously and brilliantly. Charis never ceased to marvel at the miraculous cures he had effected. His eye operations alone were already attracting patients from deep in the jungles. Three in every thousand in this country were blind. It was a wide open field for service.

Dr. Townsend never operated until first he had prayer. It was always a thrilling moment just before the anesthetic was given, when Robert, already white coated and scrubbed for the operation, folded his hands simply like a child and prayed over the patient for divine help.

The wards themselves resembled large Sunday school rooms. There was even an old magic lantern slide projector. Since few of their patients left before ten days, they had worked out a ten day course on the life of Christ. They projected the slides on the whitewashed hospital walls, and in some wards when necessary they used the ceilings.

Even the cards for each patient were painstakingly filed. The ones who appeared interested in the gospel message they had heard while in the hospital were placed in a special section. And native pastors in the areas did follow-up work on these patients when they were discharged.

Robert made no apology for using his hospital as a strong evangelistic fort. He was glad to give "a cup of cold water" to any who needed it. But he never failed to give it in Christ's name. No other motive was strong enough to have brought him to this jungle spot to minister to these people. Certainly now, with all the pressure of his own life pushing him toward a more lucrative and easy field, only God could keep him here.

He completed his morning check of patients earlier than usual, and went into the operating room to look at the list of operations scheduled for the day. It was when he went into the adjacent drug room to check on some needs that he stumbled over Charis lying on the cement floor.

A quick superficial check showed him that she was still breathing, but her respiration was slow. Her face was flushed and dusky; her lips were blue. And the pupils of her eyes were contracted to pinpoints. A quick glance at the codeine bottle in the drug cabinet confirmed his worst fears. "Oh God, don't take Charis — not this way, please, dear God . . . ."

There was little time. He carried her into the operating room. Frantically he worked with the stomach pump. Anugra's shadow fell across his shoulder.

"Quick! Get the inhalator ready, oxygen with carbon dioxide." Anugra was beside him in a moment. After they applied the mask to Charis' face the two of them stood silently by and watched and prayed. Robert was glad that Anugra asked no questions. Her anxiety showed only in the fact that she prayed like a child, aloud.

If she dies, thought Robert, *I will never forgive myself.*

I should have seen this coming for she has been dangerous to herself a long time now. It is just that between attacks she has always seemed normal, busy and good about discharging her duties. If only I had seen Dr. Glendenning sooner and arranged an earlier transfer for Charis to Burrapur.

The eyelids fluttered then closed again. But her color was better. Her hand pushed feebly at the inhalator. She would live. But she would need help as never before now that she had tried to do this dreadful thing to herself. *God, give me wisdom,* he prayed. *The right words to say. The right thing to do.*

"Robert," she called.

"I am here, Charis."

She started to cry deep, ugly sobs, like an animal. Each sob tore him apart. He literally dug his nails into his hands to keep from taking her into his arms.

"Will God ever forgive me?" was all she said.

"On Saturday," he said crisply, "I am going to drive you to the railway and you are to be on the night train for the hills. You are to go to see Dr. Kersten at the Himalayan Hospital as soon as you arrive, and you are not to return here until he discharges you. Until that time you are to occupy a hospital bed here. That is an order. Do you hear me, Charis?"

She did not answer.

"Shall I get the cart and move her into a hospital bed, Doctor Sahib?" Anugra asked. He nodded his head.

"I am so ashamed," Charis began to repeat like a broken record.

"Job once prayed," Robert's voice vibrated with sympathy as he quoted, " 'Oh, that I might have my request; and that God would grant me the things that I long for! Even that it would please God to destroy me; that He would let loose His hand, and cut me off.' Even Job, whom God Himself called 'a perfect man,' prayed for death."

"But Job had lost all his children, his possessions and his health," she answered.

"It is sometimes harder never to have had children and possessions and health."

"Thank you, Robert," she said simply. "I shall never forget that I have tried to break the sixth commandment. You have saved me from that."

CHAPTER 14

ROBERT STOOD ON THE DUSTY station platform beside some water buffaloes and waited for the train to leave. It was already four hours late, an hour or two more would scarcely matter. He had been fortunate to be able to locate a small second class compartment for Charis and Dr. Glendenning. He was grateful that this travel companion for Charis could be arranged. A saner, more comfortable, more motherly woman he had never known — and like most doctors, shock proof. For the first time in months he felt relieved. Charis Brown was in the best of hands.

The women called out of the compartment window, urging him not to wait any longer. And since he was anxious to reach Surrak Annund before nightfall, he climbed into his jeep and started his thirty-mile trek back. The women watched until the cloud of dust he raised had disappeared, then turned to make themselves as comfortable as possible.

There were four bunks in their narrow room. The other two were still unoccupied. There was no way of locking the compartment, but a latch at the foot of the door served to keep it closed while the train was stationary. But once it started on its rough, rocky way the choppy up and down movement would often spring open the feeble latch. Dr. Glendenning decided to stay awake until they had passed Katni. If at all possible on this trip she wanted to be alone. The latch — upheld also by her big booming voice — would serve to keep out the yelling trampling hordes, most of whom were third class passengers or hitchhikers.

She opened her *bhister*, rolled it out and propped up a pillow. "We may as well stretch out, Charis. If the train becomes more crowded later, they may pile in the windows, and we may scarcely have sitting space." As they were occupied with these chores the train gave a lurch and started.

It always seemed to Dr. Glendenning, as she watched the landscape slowly go by, that she could run as fast as the average Indian express train. The conductor's face appeared suddenly outside the window. She gave him their tickets; he punched them, seeming to hold on to the train only by his toes, then swung on by, walking like a fly on the outside of the corridorless train to the next compartment. Dr. Glendenning walked across the length of their narrow compartment to the opposite window, and turning to Charis said, "We have a number of free passengers in the third class next door. Come! Take a look!"

There clinging to the window ledges — on the opposite side from that along which the conductor was so skillfully weaving his way — were six passengers. As soon as the conductor moved out of sight they scrambled back into their compartment.

When she had first come to India Dr. Glendenning had always gone third class, as she used to say, humorously, "Because there is no fourth." *It must be my age,* she thought, *to make me invest a fraction of my small salary in second class travel, and feel it worthwhile.* In the third class compartment, on crowded days, passengers piled in two deep. The natives would sit cross-legged, one on the hard wooden bench and one in the aisle where normally one's feet would go. Some would stand, usually the wives of the passengers. Dr. Glendenning had been amused once to see a European gentleman rise to give an Indian woman his seat, and then see the woman's husband take it.

The unaccompanied women would huddle together in compartments reserved for women only. It was a foolish custom, for any robbers on the train would be certain of both a fertile and safe field of operation. The women were traveling banks, for they wore the family wealth in jewels on their bodies. Their husbands invested in nose rings, in silver or gold anklets, in necklaces or beaded forehead ornaments, but mostly in countless finger rings.

She had read that only the week before a wealthy woman had been killed. She had been one of thirty crowded in the *women's only* compartment. The professional thief had not even bothered to strip her rings from her fingers; he had simply hacked them off and taken them along. It paid to sleep with one eye open, and the latch and windows tightly closed.

Charis crawled on top of her open *bhister* and relaxed gratefully against the soft pillow, and on the clean sheets. Even the hot parched air seemed to be sweetened, reaching her over the clean linen. It would be a long trip, four days and four nights, before they reached the hills, and they would have to make two train changes. She looked across at her traveling companion, the only mother she had ever known. Dr. Glendenning was everyone's mother; all the Indians, even the adults, called her Mama-ji.

"I'm so glad you could come with me, Mama-ji."

Dr. Glendenning settled back on her pillow before she spoke, "What is Marjorie Townsend like?"

Charis flushed at the abrupt question, "She is like the angel on top of the Christmas tree."

"I have seen her. I asked you what is she like?"

When Charis did not answer, she was more precise, "What I am asking, is, is she as shallow as she appears to be? Is her personality as flat as the angel on the Christmas tree? Is that what you mean?"

Charis avoided a direct reply. "She did not want to be a missionary. Now that she is here I don't think she has changed her mind."

"The women men marry! What did Robert see in her?"

Charis refused to comment.

"Charis, are you in love with Robert?"

The question was like a knife which lanced deep within to reach a sore that had been festering. Charis flinched, but did not speak.

"Is that why you tried to take your life?" Seeing the hurt look on Charis' face she went on, "Robert did not tell me willingly. I dug it out of him. I am good at prying. I know you, Charis. You forget I have known you since you took your first breath. Were you pronouncing the sentence of death upon yourself because you felt you deserved it?"

"I have never thought it through," Charis whispered. "I have never let myself."

"I gave you your first spanking when you entered this world. I think you are due for another one. You have been thinking too much of yourself. Have you ever stopped to think

— if you had been successful in your suicide attempt — what it would have meant to the mission enterprise? Even the worst Hindu will think twice before he steps on an insect. And what of Robert? You are worrying him. You are on his mind. You may even be on his heart. And Charis Brown! You have no right there.

"When I came to the mission field as a young girl, my dear, a veteran male missionary told me to remember two things that every single missionary ought to know: First of all, to remember that I had volunteered to go out alone. If I did not have the strength to live alone, the mission field was no place for me.

"'If you do need help,' he told me with a twinkle in his eye, 'don't borrow male shoulders to weep on.'

"And the second thing he said was, 'Never sympathize with a married man. All married men are misunderstood, even me! Don't lend your shoulder to him!' I thought he was being funny at the time. Now I realize that he was a wise old man.

"Missionaries are not yet translated saints. Every problem we have in the homeland is only intensified in the mission field because the very geographical nature of the work binds our personalities together inextricably. We can't run away from our temptations. I should have seen this happening to you. I should have spanked you sooner."

Charis closed her eyes as she listened. Spanking was too mild a word. She felt as if she had been on an operating table without an anesthetic. She was one big hurt. She had needed the operation. She had had a good surgeon. She was glad it was over. She only hoped the operation had been successful and that the incision would heal, would form a scar.

Beneath her she heard the rhythmic beat of the wheels. She looked across at her companion. Her lecture ended, Dr. Glendenning was propped up reading a book which bobbed up and down in her hands. Charis was watching its hypnotic movement when she fell into a deep sleep, the kind she had forgotten existed.

CHAPTER 15

THE TRAIN WAS EVIDENTLY in a station when Charis awakened. She could hear the familiar cry of the venders. And the heat, now that the movement of the train had stopped, was intense. Dr. Glendenning was nowhere in sight. Charis got up and started to roll up her bedding when the door opened and her friend came in accompanied by a white turbaned servant carrying a steaming tray. The two settled down to enjoy a hearty breakfast while the train huffed and puffed and discharged and took on freight.

"There are advantages to this slow schedule," said Dr. Glendenning cheerfully, "for in a land that knows no dining cars we can still eat and eat well."

"Mmm," said Charis, drinking a sip from the deliciously brewed tea.

"Charis," said her friend, "you've never seen the Taj Mahal; and I can never see it too often. Would you like to stop at Agra on our way to the hills?"

"Oh, could we break journey and detour past it?" asked Charis eagerly.

"Agra will be frightfully hot, but no worse than Burrapur. If we arrive in time we can see the Taj by moonlight. It should be full moon tonight."

"Have you ever read by Indian moonlight, Mama-ji?"

"No, I value my eyes," replied the good doctor. "But I hear it can be done."

"When I was a little girl, and was sent off to bed early each night, I just waited for moonlight nights so that I could read in bed."

"Well, I will consent to let you ruin your eyes tonight with the guide book." She knelt by her suitcase and took out and handed the book to Charis.

Charis flipped the pages until she came to the section on Agra. "The Taj Mahal," she read, "was built during the time of Charles I of England, when the earliest European settlers were crossing the Atlantic to found the American colonies."

"Spare me the details. You bone up on the facts, dear. As many times as I have heard the guide intone its glories I should know my Taj by heart."

They spent the rest of the day happily making plans for their anticipated trip. They were so interested in this project that they forgot to close their windows when their train began to steam into the monkey station. As the hordes of monkeys started to clamber in, Dr. Glendenning chased them out. Charis was not much help, for the sight of the fat doctor chasing a grinning, chattering, mischievous monkey who expertly dodged her slaps reduced her to a state of helpless laughter.

When the last monkey had been evacuated and the windows slammed shut Charis rebuked her, "Think how disrespectful you have been to someone's mother or grandmother, Mama-ji."

"This idea of transmigration of souls has not only moral but practical drawbacks. Had you ever heard, Charis, that there is a hotel in Calcutta that pays people to sleep in unoccupied beds so that the bedbugs may be fed?"

Charis laughed. "No, but I did read recently that the Hindus have started a society called 'The Mitigation for the Monkey Nuisance.'"

"Good," said Dr. Glendenning. "I hope I can become a charter member."

They had to take a shuttle train to reach Agra, and the women were dirty and tired when they arrived that evening. But when the moon rose and shone in all its brilliance they found they did not want to be wise and wait any longer to see the famous tomb. Exhilarated with anticipation they ordered a *tonga* for their excursion. Postponement even until morning, although sensible, did not seem desirable.

And so it was by moonlight that Charis first saw this wonder of the world. The fountains were playing, and the moonlight softly illuminated the lovely marble dome and the four graceful minarets.

"Make it beautiful, as she was beautiful. Make it delicate as she was delicate. Make it graceful as she was graceful." She remembered the command of the Emperor Shah Jehan to his Persian architect. "Usted Isa succeeded, didn't he, Mama-ji? He captured as he was ordered to do, the spirit of Arjemand, Mumtaz Mahal, Chosen of the Palace, in stone."

Dr. Glendenning had stood aside to allow Charis to have this moment of beauty alone. Now she made only a practical observation, "It took twenty-two thousand workers twenty-two years to build the Taj Mahal. Usted Ali, the architect — if we can believe the reports — was blinded by order of the Shah so that never again should a rival thing of beauty be created."

Charis shivered. "Why in India must every beautiful thing be bathed in blood?"

"They say," continued her friend, "that the Shah planned to build a black marble mosque across the river for himself as his mausoleum and join the two by an ivory bridge. But his son, with his eyes on the family coffers, imprisoned the old man for the last seven years of his life, and that dream was never realized. His son had reason to fear the extravagance of his father. It was his father, you know, who first sat on the famous Peacock Throne, which was studded with the most enormous jewels ever seen. And ten thousand pearls are woven into the canopy that was folded over the casket of the Shah's favorite wife."

"She was only one of many?" asked Charis.

"Her name indicated what she was, 'Favorite of the Palace or Chosen of the Palace.'"

"And yet how strange in a land where a woman is usually on a level lower than a beast, to find this lovely tomb, built for a woman. It is a symbol of love."

"I like to call it a monarch's extravagant tear."

"I like that, Dr. Glendenning. It is just that, a beautiful fragile teardrop."

They sat in the formal gardens and watched the water play. It was finally the practical doctor who remembered the waiting *tonga* and who made the first move to leave. "We will come back again and see it by daylight. But there will never be a moment in your life, my dear, to equal this first glimpse of its beauty."

As they lay tucked in their beds in the mission hostel Charis, still filled with the magic of the moment, turned to her friend, "Mama-ji, is love once felt never realized again?"

"An English professor of mine, an old maid, used to say to

every class to which she taught *Romeo and Juliet* — incidentally, she would punctuate every important remark with a sniff, so that you always knew when to make notes — 'Romeo and Juliet is not what I would classify as a real tragedy. They found each other. Sniff . . . sniff . . . sniff. The only real love tragedy is never to find the one you love.'"

"Then she believed that there is only one man for one woman."

"Yes, but she like most spinsters was incurably romantic and wrong!"

"Mama-ji!"

"Another professor of mine would say to every class he taught in family relationships that any two Christian people could fall in love after marriage and make a wonderful and happy Christian home if they were willing to work at it."

"You agree with him."

"No, not entirely. But I lean more to his viewpoint. I once read a book — not a medical textbook — but a novel. I remember nothing about it but one scene in which the heroine after a sad love affair is trying to make herself marry a suitable young man who is in love with her. She almost succeeds in persuading herself into this match when a trifling thing upset her plans. He uses the washroom in her apartment. After he leaves she washes her face and hands and reaches for a towel. She cannot bring herself to use the same towel he has used."

Charis laughed.

"She doesn't marry the man, I believe. And I am sure she shouldn't have. So if you want my views, let's just say I believe that any two Christian people who can use the same towel can live happily ever after. And now, my dear, good night!"

CHAPTER 16

IT WAS DIFFICULT TO DECIDE what made Indian travel most distressing. Sometimes Charis thought it was the tiny inhabitants that lived tucked away in the corners of the seats, hungry lice, starved fleas and related pests that greedily feasted on her skin. Some people seemed to possess that dubious quality of being attractive to these invaders. Charis had always been popular with them. In spite of her adept thumb catching and annihilating a great many, often too many penetrated her guard, and journey's end found her a mass of unbearably itchy welts.

Another major annoyance was the way in which people never learned to allow passengers to alight before crowding in. Every station, when one was in a crowded compartment, developed into a battlefield. People trying to get off shrieked, yelled and occasionally flung fists or clubs in order to push out the solid door of incoming passengers in a vain effort to get out. It was perhaps as well the trains stayed long in each station or too many of the feebler ones would be carried on beyond their destinations.

But even more distressing to her was the army of beggars who attacked at every station. The railway was their most lucrative field of operation. Even though one realized that their cripplings were often self-mutilations, one was filled with pity and loathing. They were so importunate in their pleas, and fought and crawled through the crowds to the most plausible benefactors, and if at all possible touched the shoes of the importuned. Charis, in spite of a lifetime spent in the Orient, shrank from this contact. Lepers, maimed, blind, all used their diseases for their trade. In one section one even saw human beings with grotesquely shaped heads. Some children of the beggar caste here had their growing heads placed in long jars to make them grow deformed in this attenuated way. The children grew up idiotic, but they were great objects of pity and the recipients of much alms.

The stations were places of strange sights and sounds and smells, mostly unpleasant. But once the train wheels set in motion, if one were fortunate enough to have the privacy of a compartment, and if one had been successful in a delousing job, it was relaxing to see the rice fields of the plains pass, the village children standing to watch the trains move by, waving as children of all ages and all countries will always do. The skyline challenged the imagination with an occasional silhouette of a mosque or a temple and less frequently a church spire. There was a certain peace to be found in the rhythmic shaking of the train. It was good to be the one who was moving, rather than an observer watching the world go by. Charis guessed this was what people must mean by the therapeutic value of travel.

Charis had fallen asleep hot and sticky from the atmosphere of the plains. During the night on their fourth day of travel the train had come to its journey's end at the station of Bereilly in the foothills of the Himalayas. She awakened to feel the cool snow washed air of the mountains on her face.

Dr. Glendenning was leaning out the window to make arrangements for their transfer to the smaller gauge train that would take them further up the mountains. Then their last lap of the journey would have to be by taxi, straight up the curving mountain roads.

As they followed the porter the doctor had engaged to carry their luggage they passed a group of nuns climbing into an Indian *tonga*. They were no doubt going to their mission station in Bereilly.

"Sometimes," Dr. Glendenning said, "I envy them their garb; but not at moments like these." One of the sisters had caught her long robe on a protruding edge of the two wheeled cart, and was having trouble extricating herself without losing that dignity which seemed so much a part of these women.

Charis smiled. "Why would you of all people want to wear a garb?"

The doctor replied seriously, "Because it lends a certain dignity to the celibate life. It is as if that habit they wear proclaims to the world that the wearer has deliberately turned her back on the pleasures of the world, has chosen a manless world. Now take us. Who would believe that even I, with a face like mine, had my chances at matrimony, that I preferred to be a single missionary?

"I get fed up with the constant jeering at old maids. It isn't just the Catholic faith that believes there is a singular place for the single in Christian service, but the Roman Church has dignified its adherents by placing them in orders and setting them apart in communities of their own. But Protestants have in their own open Bible these words, 'There is a difference also between a wife and a virgin. The unmarried woman careth for the things of the Lord, that she may be holy both in body and in spirit; but she that is married careth for the things of the world, how she may please her husband.' Many of us have deliberately chosen to dedicate our lives to singleness of heart, to one love, the love of God, that we may please Him. We, too, have taken the vow of chastity for life for Christ's sake. And I do wish there were some way of raising our service above the level of the jest."

Charis looked in surprise at her friend, "I never knew you felt any stigma in your unmarried status."

"We all feel it, even the least sensitive of us. Social life is patterned for married people. It is difficult to feel at ease in a social mixed group — even for a doctor. Especially here in India where bachelors are practically non-existent. These nuns are spared these contacts, and I am sure are happier for them. There is no stigma to being single. It is just plain human vanity, I guess, that makes me want to wear a sign, 'I chose to be single.' I have never regretted my choice. I wouldn't give up my precious Indian family for any of my own flesh and blood. Oh, I have moments when I long for closer human relationships, but when I do I just say to myself, 'Why should you have what Jesus Himself never had, *Miss* Glendenning?' and it works. And it was Christ Himself who said, "Everyone that hath forsaken houses, or brethren, or sisters, or father, or mother, or wife, or children, or lands, for my name's sake, shall receive an hundredfold'! "

Dr. Glendenning's philosophizing was ended by the coolie's arrival at the new train, and all her energy was taken up with the customary haggling over the money owed the luggage carrier. She listened stonily while she heard of the twelve hungry motherless children he possessed. The give and take lasted all of five minutes. When they had both beaten each other down sufficiently, money exchanged hands, and the triumphant doctor heaved her large bulk with a sigh into the seat opposite Charis.

Charis reopened the subject, "And what of us who have not deliberately chosen this life of walking alone, who have never had a chance to turn our backs on home and kindred for Christ's sake? Shall we receive an hundredfold?"

Dr. Glendenning looked sympathetically across at the young face of this child who was like her own.

Charis pressed on wistfully, "Is there any virtue to a state that is not self chosen?"

"No," replied the doctor. "None at all. But the Bible can speak to you, too. First of all, like Paul you must learn 'In whatsoever state I am, therewith to be content.' Then in time, if it is God's plan that you remain unmarried you will rejoice in His providence that will permit you to serve Him with a singleness of heart. And believe me, my dear, your hundredfold blessings begin then even in this life."

"*Nagpuri cuntra! Nagpuri cuntra!*" called the vender at their carriage window.

"I don't believe it," said Charis. She leaned out the window and bought a dozen of the oranges. They peeled like tangerines and inside oozed with sweet juice. She bit into one. "They are! They are Nagpuri cuntra! Oranges from home!" It was just the beginning of her vacation and already she was homesick for the plains.

Dr. Glendenning peeled her orange and with her booming voice began to sing "The Hills of Home." Charis smiled while her companion sang, "I miss the broken skyline that I know." When she had finished, however, she in turn quoted from "The Plains" by Laurence Hope:

> How one loves them
> Those wide horizons; whether Desert or Sea —
> Vague and vast and infinite . . . .

Dr. Glendenning did not let her finish, but continued to boom loudly and slightly off pitch the glories of the "Hills of Home."

The train jerked to a start. The plains unraveled behind them until at last before and beside and above them towered only the hills.

CHAPTER 17

AFTERWARDS IT HAD ALWAYS seemed to Charis that the tragedy would have been more bearable if there had been some ominous warning or some dark foreshadowing of the event. Instead, the whole trip had been rich with love, laughter and beauty. It seemed incredible that these days which Charis would always treasure in her heart had such a cruel end.

It happened that night while they were still chugging toward Khatgodam, the end of the railway, that the marauder had entered their compartment. Every other night they had taken precaution to close doors and windows. Ironically, it was the temptation to enjoy the cool mountain air that had made them leave the window open.

It was Charis who awakened to sense the figure standing beside her bed. A quick glance across the compartment showed her that the body of her friend was still in her bunk. She screamed and flung herself sideways even as the knife slashed down. It missed her and she grappled in a life and death struggle with the man who she could tell from the well-oiled body was a professional thief and murderer.

His greasy body broke through every hold she got. She did not know when Dr. Glendenning entered the fight. She only felt the pressure against her throat released, and fighting free she frantically grabbed for the emergency chain with which she could halt the train. As she fell with the sudden application of the train's brakes, the man stepped over her body and disappeared out the window.

"Mama-ji! Mama-ji!"

There was no answer. Running footsteps came outside her carriage. Someone was carrying a lantern. She opened the door and by its light they found the doctor. She was crumpled up at the foot of the bed, and bleeding profusely from several knife wounds in the chest.

The rest of the night was full of choppy fragments. She remembered getting the doctor back on her open *bhister* and trying to staunch the gaping wounds. The engineer, knowing there was no turnaround track for miles, had backed the train all the way to Bereilly. Everyone had been wonderfully kind. But even as she sat beside her friend, Charis knew there was no hope. Only a blood transfusion would help the doctor, keep her alive. And they would not reach Bereilly in time.

Why? Why? Why? Her thoughts turned with each revolution of the wheels. *Here I seek death, and it eludes me. Yet when it comes unasked I dodge the blade of the knife. And because I scream the most wonderful woman in the world is dead. And I sit here, unscathed, a living breathing wreck of humanity. Why? Oh, why?*

The doctor died without regaining consciousness, without saying a word. The police discovered that the thief had taken her purse. It had contained twelve rupees. For the sake of three dollars this invaluable life had been snuffed out.

They buried the doctor in Bereilly within sight of the hills of home, and Charis took the next train back for the plains.

CHAPTER 18

ROBERT WAS GLAD TO BE DRIVING back to Surrak Annund alone. He had left Dhunwa in the city to pick up grocery supplies which he would accompany home the following day by buffalo cart. The jeep did not seem able to travel fast enough in the deeply rutted roads to escape its own dust. He choked and finally stopped until the whirling cloud he had raised settled, it seemed regretfully, about him.

He had always imagined the jungle to be cool and green with running streams and tall trees that tangled into a roof above the wayfarer. There were roads running out from Surrak Annund which approached this image; but the jungle between it and Burrapur was sparse, scrubby and dusty. Yet he knew that even here there was danger from the jungle beasts. He did not care to be in an open jeep after dark, and so he grimly started up his motor again and choked and coughed his way along.

There were four streams to ford. In the rainy season each presented a threat. Today their riverbeds were almost dry. It was only necessary for him to shift into his most powerful gear and plow through the sand. It was as he started through the last *nulla* that he was halted by a group of villagers. They were delighted to see him, for they were carrying on a flat native bed a man who obviously needed emergency attention.

He stepped down from the jeep and going over looked at the deep lacerations on the man's legs. They told him the fantastic story that he had received them in a wrestling match with a panther.

It seemed the man and his young son were out with bow and arrow after small game when an unexpected panther had appeared and turned the hunter into the hunted. The panther had been too close to enable the father to use his bow and arrow; so calling to his son to hide behind a tree, he had in desperation taken on the beast with his bare hands. Twice the

75

panther sprang. And twice the man dodged. Then before the beast sprang the third time the man catapulted himself through the air. Man and panther had met in mid-air, and the man had, by the very surprise element in his attack, been able to throw the big cat on its back. As he did so, however, the panther had embedded his rear claws into the man's thighs and ripped his legs to shreds. Facing death, the father held on grimly to the throat of the beast, and calling to his son had ordered him to deliver the death stroke by thrusting a spear into the writhing animal.

Robert set up an emergency hospital on the spot, and using his medical kit, which was always with him, he carefully disinfected and sutured the wounds. No white man could survive such a mauling but the natives seemed immune to tetanus, the main danger from the wicked claws. As he worked over the man the villagers told him that the slowness of the rains, and the death of many forest animals, were driving these feared jungle beasts to seek food by preying on the village cattle and sheep. They spoke with terror of a newly appeared menace, a maneating tiger.

He had mauled and partly eaten a little village boy who was herding a small flock of goats. It was unusual to attack the boy rather than the goats, for the unflattering fact was that the average tiger preferred animal meat to human flesh. But the natives said that when a tiger became old and his teeth fell out he could no longer enjoy the gamy meat of the jungle, which he preferred. Then he sought out a soft diet, and became a dreaded maneater.

The shadows were falling, and the villagers became uneasy. A *nulla*, or watering hole, was no place to be with a maneating tiger on the prowl. As Robert finished his bandaging he insisted that the man must be carried the rest of the way to the hospital that night for further care. That they refused to do. And in desperation Robert promised if they would walk ahead he would drive the jeep behind them all the way and protect them with his lights and his gun. They were reassured and with complete confidence the procession continued.

There was no way of notifying Marjorie of this unavoidable delay. No runner would dare go ahead alone with the news. All he could do was crawl along at this snail's pace. There was no way he could keep his promise to her to be back by nightfall.

SONG BY THE RIVER

The night was very black. There would be a moon later if the clouds permitted it to break through. Charis and Dr. Glendenning should be at Lucknow by this time. He envied them the trip to the hills.

His mind swung back and forth thinking of the two women. In the end his concern for Marjorie was swallowed up by his greater anxiety and hope that Charis could find healing for her mind in this needed rest.

The natives ahead started to sing loudly to frighten away the beasts and the evil spirits. They sang in unison, with a pounding rhythm. They left the jungle blackness behind them as the lights of the jeep tore open the miles of black velvet which lay ahead.

CHAPTER 19

MARJORIE HAD BEEN DISAPPOINTED not to be able to go to the station with Charis. The infrequent trips to the headquarters on the railroad represented the only contact that the Surrak Annund station had with the outside world. In the intervening months they lived in isolation in their jungle clearing. But Robert had not permitted her to drive in the jeep over the rough thirty miles of road which had been hewn out of the jungle. Whatever his personal interest in the new life she carried might be, he did not fail to insist that she obey all the medical decisions he made.

Marjorie decided to fill her day with a social visit to the Rani Sahib. She found these visits of hers an escape from reality, and thought of the palace as a land of enchantment. It would be a lack of good taste, however, to go unannounced, and so she sent Babu-ji ahead to make the necessary approach. She did not have long to wait before the Rani's servant arrived to escort her to the palace.

The Rajah was away inspecting some of his northern villages, and the Rani was lonely and as eager as she for the unexpected visit. It was interesting, thought Marjorie, how the Indian woman's whole life centered in her husband. Men in India were always the pivot around which domestic life revolved. As girls, fathers were the gods of the home. As wives, husbands were objects of worship. Even as older women, the male domination still continued. This time it was the sons who occupied the pedestal.

Whenever the Rajah was away, for the Rani the clock stopped. She was obviously happy, today, to fill her empty hours with her American friend. The two shook hands with delight, and settled down to enjoy the sweetmeats and other spicy delicacies which a woman attendant brought. They managed to carry on a spirited conversation in Hindii, in English, but mostly with the use of hands.

The Rani's first question, as always, was about the state of the unborn child. Marjorie sensed that her value had greatly increased in the eyes of her friend when her own pregnancy had become apparent. And it became evident to Marjorie that her friend was increasingly distressed by her own prolonged childlessness.

The Rajah showed no wavering in his devotion to his girl bride; but in time both women knew there would be the question of the succession to the *Raj* or kingdom. And even more important there was the underlying fear of damnation which hung as a present threat over the Rajah. For if there should be no son to carry on the family line, the Rajah upon his death would be damned; and not only he, but the whole line of ancestors from which he sprang. The word for boy, *putra,* Marjorie knew, meant "deliverer from hell." The word, *put,* literally translated, meant hell; and *ra* stood for deliverer.

Marjorie felt the envy of her friend, and wished she could persuade her to come to the hospital for help. But much as Sundri wanted a child and spoke openly of her longing, this possibility lay beyond consideration. The only time Robert had ever been called to the palace for his medical opinion on the Rani, he had had to prescribe medication on the basis of a diagnosis made from a wrist extended around the latticed screen. One look at the hand had made it quite evident that it was the hand of a servant girl.

Sundri clapped her hands, as they exchanged their opening inquiries, and a servant girl appeared carrying on a brass tray a lovely blue sari trimmed with gold thread. It was a present for Marjorie. She exclaimed with delight as the servant girl showed her how to drape it about herself. *What a wonderful maternity dress,* she thought. One could remain slender and lovely until the end, for the sari fell in soft concealing folds about her. She loved wearing it, and settled back against the cushions, enveloped in the soft silk and surrounded by the heady smell of the sandalwood ointment the Rani used, to enjoy the afternoon.

The conversation went on in its usual cycle of husbands, children, food, reverting always back to husbands. There was a prescribed limit to the range of subjects that interested the Rani. She undoubtedly had majored all her life in the course on how to please a husband. She never stirred far afield from the subject. *It is a course I have neglected to take,* thought Marjorie. *How far apart we are in our outlook.*

But today Marjorie sensed an undercurrent of worry in Sundri whenever she referred to the Rajah. Even her visit was cut short because the Rani had to take her ceremonial bath and do *puja* — worship — at the temple which had been erected for her in the courtyard.

Marjorie knew that this bath was always a necessity, for she by her presence necessitated it. The Rani needed ceremonial purification after her association with a person not of her caste. But of late this temple worship had become an obsession with her. *My contact with her,* thought Marjorie, *has not helped. She is further from Christ and deeper in Hinduism.*

As she wandered by the elephant stables and past the temple on her way out of the palace ground, she stopped for the first time to examine the carved images of the gods which surrounded its base. The gestures and postures of many of the gods and goddesses were obscene. How horrible to think her friend thought help for her barrenness could come from such as these. She found the veil of enchantment which surrounded her visits to the palace smutted by this contact, this facet of her friend's life she preferred usually to ignore. And she found herself comparing her own life with that of the little Rani. How would she feel, and how would she fare if Robert were a Hindu?

It was lonely at dinner eating by herself. She felt uneasy. She seldom stayed depressed long, but this evening Robert's continued absence, and the unhappy conclusion of her visit to the palace, prolonged her mood. And when night fell with its usual swiftness, and Robert had still not returned, she felt overcome with a feeling of apprehension. It did not help her state of mind to realize that there was nothing she could do but wait.

She could not bring herself, however, to undress and go to bed, but curled up instead on the divan in the living room. As she blew out her lamp, the sight of the watchman with his lantern on the veranda comforted her. She lay wide-eyed and awake, watching, and straining her ears for the first sound of the returning jeep. She must have slept, for when she awakened the lantern had gone out. She could see nothing. Fear, then terror possessed her. She felt she must escape the suffocating blackness. It was then she heard the scream. It was no jungle scream this time, but human — yet scarcely human. Some last shred of sense sent her plunging through the darkness for the duftar and the guns.

As she clutched a rifle to her, the night became silent around her. There were no more screams; there was no sound. No power on earth could drive her to investigate the now silent terror. She did not know how long she stood before she heard the jeep clatter into the compound. Still she did not move. It was only when she heard Robert call her name that she groped her way back to the living room to open the door.

It was still black outside, and blacker within. And she only realized that she still held the gun when Robert struck a match and lit the lamp on the piano.

"Marjorie, the gun, why the gun?"

Incoherently she managed to tell of the terror that had been. He did not wait for her to finish, but grabbing the gun from her, he took the lamp in his other hand and rushed outdoors. She stood again enveloped in complete darkness. Robert did not return. She must have stood there until the dawn.

It was from the punkha boy she heard, finally, what had happened. A maneating tiger had mauled the night watchman. The doctor sahib had carried him to the hospital, but he was already dead. There was no blame in the boy's eyes as he prosaically stated the facts. No native would have acted otherwise. She had behaved normally, native fashion. Robert had still not returned. And Marjorie felt now that she was glad. She did not want to see him, for she knew what his eyes would reveal.

She had had an arsenal of guns at hand. She had heard the cry of a human in distress. And she had cowered in the safety of her home, with a gun in her hand, and let a beast tear a fellow human being to death on her doorstep.

"It was not my fault," she reasoned with herself. "The watchman was supposed to be on duty, and he slept. He slept at his post. He must not have checked his lantern for oil. The light went out. No jungle animal would come near light. It was his fault — his, not mine, not mine!" But none of the reasons she frantically sought would satisfy Robert, she knew that; and with a cold fatalism, she faced the fact that none of them would even satisfy herself.

CHAPTER 20

IT WAS AN INAUSPICIOUS BEGINNING for their days alone together. Robert had not commented on the incident and Marjorie had been afraid to open the subject. Their mealtime conversation, now dependent on their mutual interests alone, sputtered and died. It was almost as if the absence of Charis only augmented the distance which had grown between them.

One evening after Marjorie's weekly visit to the palace her growing concern over her friend's unhappiness led her to seek Robert's advice and ultimately it was this which led to the graver ignored situation between them. Marjorie had begun with the question, "Do you think there is any likelihood that the Rajah will divorce his wife because of her childlessness?"

Robert frowned before he answered. "I doubt it very much. He is European in his outlook on women. Is Sundri Rani concerned?"

"She doesn't speak about it," Marjorie answered. "But all her usual animation seems gone. And the Rajah has been away now from the palace for six weeks. It is the longest absence from him that she has known."

"The grounds for a Hindu divorce — limited incidentally to the man — as found in their religious book the *Puranas* is: 'A barren wife may be superseded in the eighth year. A woman who bears only daughters in the ninth. A woman whose children all die in the tenth. And a quarrelsome woman without delay.' The Rajah has only been married four years. Unless she is quarrelsome," he smiled, "Sundri's time has not run out. Her anxiety must have some other basis."

"The Rajah is such a wonderful man. He told me that he leaned toward a Christian philosophy. The more I see of him the more I feel he is a Christian in his heart."

Robert raised his eyebrows. "Is it possible to be a believer without confessing Christ?"

"Robert! How could you expect him to confess his faith? If he did you know he would lose his kingdom, maybe even his life. Could you expect such a sacrifice from him?"

"And what shall it profit a man, if he gain the whole world and lose his own soul?" Robert quoted.

"But think," Marjorie continued, "think of how wisely he has ruled all his villages. It would be a betrayal of the faith his people have in him if he were forced to abdicate for religious reasons."

"The end, Marjorie, never justifies the means."

"I just feel very deeply that God will never condemn such a good man."

"There is none righteous, no not one."

"I wish you would stop quoting, quoting, quoting." Marjorie's voice was edged. "I am convinced the Rajah is a secret believer."

"No man," said Robert, "can know about another soul's eternal destiny in this life with any finality. Only the last days will reveal to us who is truly saved. The only criteria we have to go by, however, is not how we feel about the matter, but what God's Word says about the subject. That is why I 'quote, quote, quote.' And I can find nothing in the Bible to sanction the idea of the possibility of secret discipleship. There is, on the other hand, much explicit Scripture on the necessity for open confession. Even our Great Commission is to go, teach and *baptize*. I can never get around the verse, 'Whosoever therefore shall confess me before men, him will I confess also before my Father which is in heaven.'"

"But doesn't God give us an inner voice to guide us? Why can't we trust our feelings in this matter?"

"We can, when they are guided by the spoken Word. But no man's conscience by itself is totally reliable. In Adam's sin our whole nature was corrupted. Not that we are totally depraved like the beasts. But there is no facet of our personality which has not been smudged by the black hand of sin. We cannot, therefore, even trust wholly this inner voice. It must be 'Thy *word* is a lamp unto my feet, and a light unto my path.'"

"Robert, was it a sin for me to let the *chowkidar* die?"

"Must we discuss it, Marjorie?"

"You feel it was."

"Yes, I do. But even in this matter I would not trust my own judgment. It doesn't matter what I feel."

"What does the Bible say about my action?"

"Do you really want to know?"

"Yes."

"I feel you violated the sixth commandment, 'Thou shalt not kill.' That commandment implies that in addition to not taking life we must do all we can to preserve life, the life of others — and our own," he added thoughtfully.

"But would I not have endangered my own by trying to preserve his? May I not have been killed myself?"

"A Christian, when a choice must be made, always prefers others to himself. 'Greater love hath no man than this that a man lay down his life for his friends.'"

But even as Robert was expounding these principles to Marjorie, he felt uneasy in his heart. Why did he withdraw from his wife when she in the interest of self-preservation broke the commandment? Why did he preach at her? When Charis had flagrantly violated the same commandment in her suicide attempt, he had felt overcome only with sorrow and charity, and had failed to rebuke her. Should he not abhor the one act as much as the other? Was subjectivity warping his sense of judgment? But were not the acts different? Marjorie lived, breathed and revolved around the pivot point of herself. Her sin was motivated by self love, self interest. On the other hand, in his years of working with Charis and watching her, he had discovered the most selfless person he knew. Her sin had been motivated by self hate. He did not need to rebuke her. Her sensitive soul without his prodding would be enduring the tortures of the damned.

But in spite of this rationalization he felt uncomfortable in his judgment, and because of it was gentler with his wife than he felt she deserved.

When she said, "I shall never forget that cry, Robert, as long as I live," he was moved to reply gently, "Some crises in life are especially difficult because they necessitate immediate action. Your whole life, Marjorie, has conditioned you to act as you did. If you had had more time to consider, even more time to pray, you might have acted differently."

"You mean, I might have risen to the occasion — is that

the correct trite phrase? Or do you mean I might have acted as a Christian?"

Robert had never seen Marjorie so self condemnatory before. *She needs help,* he thought, *she needs help from me.* But when he tried to reach out to help her involuntarily he drew back. The chasm between them he was not man enough to bridge, for now between them he saw too the cruelly mangled body of the *chowkidar.* Even as he prayed for the spirit of forgiveness, of charity, the moment passed, and Marjorie had withdrawn herself from him again into a wilderness of words.

They had had one other serious conversation between them. Marjorie was always surprising Robert with the heretical ideas she harbored. She had gone to the same Christian college, and been subjected to the same thought as he, but she seemed to have come through it in some magic manner without her thinking having been in the least affected. But even he had been jolted when they had been discussing a new holy man who had taken up his lodging under the peepul tree near the hospital.

"Surely God will save him," she had stated rather than asked.

"Why?" He was aghast.

"Robert, look at him. He scarcely eats. He lies there day and night on a bed of spikes. Look at his withered arm. He has let it become paralyzed and useless. All this in devotion to God."

"To God?"

"To the only God he knows. Why, I have never suffered for my religion the way he has, and neither have you. He is the most sincere man I have known. And see how he suffers for what he believes."

"Indian holiness, Marjorie, you will notice is never service for others. The holiest man is the one who tortures himself the most, not the one who serves others the most devotedly. But back up a bit. Did I hear you say that you thought his sincerity would save him?"

"Yes, I did. And, Robert, please don't start quoting again."

"Marjorie, this is a serious error. After all, you are a missionary's wife. I don't know how you ever slipped through the board's examination on your religious beliefs, thinking the way you do."

"Why not? I slipped through yours."

He blushed. "I just assumed you agreed with me."

"Why not confess, Robert, in those days, you weren't as interested in my mind." She spoke teasingly.

But Robert refused to see any humor in the situation. And that night for family devotions he read from the first Book of Kings and the eighteenth chapter. As he read about Elijah's contest with the prophets of Baal his voice underlined every passage which indicated the apparent sincerity of these men.

"They cried aloud, and cut themselves after their manner with knives and lancets, till the blood gushed out upon them."

And he did not eliminate to read with expression their dire end.

CHAPTER 21

ROBERT WAS MORE ANNOYED at the Saddhu's presence at the hospital gate than he cared to admit. Legally the man had a perfect right there; he was actually sitting a yard away from the property line. He caused no disturbance, in fact did not speak at all. Still, Robert knew the clinic patients who had to pass the holy man to enter the gates were disturbed by his presence. Some needy cases even stopped coming.

Typical Indian non-resistance, Robert thought. It was the passive resistance so advocated by Gandhi. The man simply sat on his bed of spikes, naked except for a shred of loincloth, his body smeared with saffron, his hair stiff with cow dung, and fingered his beads with his one good arm. The other hand he held always upright. It had withered in this position through a self-induced paralysis. How could one fight his influence?

He was angry one day to see Marjorie go out of her way to stop and look at the holy man, and even more annoyed to see her pick up his *lota* or brass cup, and take it to the well in the mission yard and fill it and take it back to him. The Saddhu seemed to be oblivious to the attention he was receiving from such a strange source. When she entered the hospital Robert reproached her.

"Why did you fill the Saddhu's drinking vessel?" His tone indicated his displeasure.

"It was empty."

"I assure you he has enough devotees of his own who amply take care of him. They bring him three meals a day — many of them who can scarcely scrape together enough for one meal for themselves."

"But he is sitting right at our gates. I feel he is our own responsibility. Perhaps he has come to us for help."

"He is there to annoy and frustrate our work. Already our

Hindu patients are dropping away. They fear the look of their holy man."

"Have you seen his eyes, Robert? There is nothing to fear in them."

"What makes you say that?"

"I looked into them. It seems to me that they are filled with nothing but compassion. They are the eyes of Jesus."

"That's blasphemous!"

"I only know he makes me ashamed. I wish I had enough love for God to sit as he does day by day . . . ."

"And what good does his self-inflicted torture do?"

"At least it makes me uncomfortable."

"I can't understand you, Marjorie. You cringe back at the slightest contact with a dirty native. You cannot bring yourself to nurse a sick, needy native patient. And yet here you are overcome with admiration over the least bathed member of our community."

Marjorie said nothing.

"Instead of sitting," Robert continued, "could not your holy man better spend his time attending the lepers and other diseased and needy beings that pass his peepul tree?"

"Is it not more worthy to spend one's days seeking God? If I may quote, 'Mary hath chosen the better part.'"

"Mary sat at the feet of our Lord."

"She had met our Lord. He was a guest in her home; she knew Him. The Saddhu is still seeking Him. He spends his days trying to find Him."

"'Seek and ye shall find.' If you are right, Marjorie, if the holy man is truly seeking Him, Christ will appear to him. Believe me, I only hope you are right, and that he is not there to make mischief. I know he is annoying not only me but some of my Moslem patients. I only hope his passive resistance will not erupt — as it too frequently does — into force and violence on the part of others."

"You do not mind if I am kind to him?"

"Should I be the one to forbid a 'cup of cold water in His name'? My only concern is that your action should not be misunderstood."

"I shall not become his follower, if that is what bothers you. But I should like to find my own peepul tree and sit and sit and sit until I too could find God."

Robert looked searchingly at his wife; seeing the earnestness in her face he picked up the Bible which always lay on his office desk, and handed it to her. "I can only repeat. The only place to find God is through His own revealed Word, in His own revealed way. By all means sit under a peepul tree; but while you are sitting you will find it more profitable to read this."

She took the book gravely from him. Robert had not reassured her that she did not need to find God, that she had already found Him. He, too, must know what she had been awakening to with a slow and relentless realization, that she did not know Him, that she was a missionary who needed to be converted.

As she left the building she picked up a tract from the rack in the hall. It was one written in Hindii and contained Bible excerpts on conversion. As her path led her by the Saddhu again, she stooped and placed the pamphlet on the ground before the man. She half expected him to tear up the tract. Instead there was no response. Only the deep melancholy eyes betrayed as usual the fact that the man was alive.

Robert watched her from the window. She looked incongruous in her pretty flowered maternity dress bending over the filthy motionless figure. Marjorie was becoming more unpredictable with each new day. He could not see from where he stood that she had given the man a tract. But he did notice the Saddhu turn his face to watch his wife as she stepped daintily down the mission path.

CHAPTER 22

MARJORIE'S BIRTHDAY WAS IN JUNE. It had always been a favorite month of hers. To her chagrin in India, although the natives considered it a propitious month for weddings, it was chiefly the month of the big monsoon. Torrents of rain fell and it seemed that overnight the parched arid soil became an oozy protoplasmic primeval slime. Even indoors one could not escape the rains. They made themselves heard either with bombastic thunderings or the more aggravating drip drip of each individual raindrop. Clothing could no longer be dried in the sun, and so molded. Marjorie noted that even her good shoes in the closet accumulated a layer of thick green mold, just from the dampness in the atmosphere.

In the village there was much rejoicing over the rains, the life-giving rains, which when they were generous watered the rice fields. Some years when the rains were overgenerous the rice was drowned and crops failed. Some years when the rains came late, the rice withered and died before it could be revived. But always life centered about the rains. This year the rains came at a propitious time and in propitious amounts. Rice crops would be good, and those who lived a hand-to-mouth existence rejoiced, for they would have full rice bowls.

But for Marjorie, to whom rice was not of primary importance, there was no cause for joy in the unrelenting steady downpours. She went to sleep at night hearing the pitter patter on the tin roof. The first sound in the morning was the same monotonous noise.

Her birthday morning was no different from any of the rest. It had started as a complete washout. Not only the weather outside contributed, but her own temerity started the day wrong. Longing for a good American birthday cake, she had finally dared to trespass on the cook's own territory, and of course

SONG BY THE RIVER

his dire predictions of failure had come true. Her cake had looked lovely when she placed it tenderly in the oven, but it had shriveled to nothing in the intense heat of the wood stove. Why didn't some kind heart prepare a cookbook for use under these sub-normal conditions? Nothing behaved the way it should. Bake forty-five minutes evidently did not mean what it said.

Robert had left for the hospital before she had awakened. At noon there was a message from him not to expect him home for lunch. Not wanting to face what could easily happen that day, and also a companyless birthday dinner, in desperation Marjorie wrote a short note to Anugra asking her to come to dinner.

Charis had had her head nurse in for dinner on a number of occasions. Marjorie had met her, and although the girl had not made any definite impression on her for good or bad, she was at least someone to turn to in this extremity.

In the end Robert had materialized in time for dinner. He was obviously happy to see Anugra an invited guest. In that quiet way by which news infiltrates the lives of all the natives on the mission compound, Anugra had learned it was Marjorie's birthday. She had brought with her, Indian fashion, a lovely lei, and then with that occidental touch which no doubt she had learned from Charis, she had brought a beautifully wrapped gift. Inside, it was a lovely silver filigree bracelet. Marjorie was enchanted with it.

Robert apologetically brought out his own gift. It was still in the newspaper in which it had been originally wrapped. It was an exquisite ring, of soft, pure, yellow Indian gold; a ringlet of tiny pearls surrounded the center stone, a blood red ruby. She slipped it on her right hand, and her childlike delight in it, as she deliberately turned her hand, letting the soft lamplight highlight the ruby, pleased Robert. Actually he had bought it for her when he had first come to India, and had kept it for a special occasion. He had not remembered his wife's birthday. This afternoon when Anugra innocently reminded him of the special day he had fortunately remembered the ring.

It had been — in spite of all the fury and noise of the rain outdoors — a cozy and intimate evening. Anugra, whom one seldom saw apart from Charis, shone in her new isolated personality. She was delightful, gracious and charming to Marjorie. Robert knew that she was responding to the utter lack of self-consciousness his wife showed over her color. Marjorie —

and for this he was glad — had never shown any trace of race superiority feelings. That she did not like the natives in India was bound up to her dislike of their habits, especially their complete indifference to hygiene, a fetish with Marjorie, and not to any dislike of their color. In college it had been a trait of Marjorie's that he had liked. They had never discussed the race question. There had been no reason to talk about it. It was merely assumed by them both that a man was to be judged apart from his skin.

Any native who came near Marjorie was aware of this in an instinctive way. How soon they learned to know those who condescended to them, or who had inner fights with themselves over the race barrier. One of the reasons Marjorie continued to be such a favorite at the palace, Robert was sure, was because the Rajah responded to this trait of his wife. He was a proud man and would not long have tolerated a superior attitude. Anugra on the other hand, in her studies for her nurse's degree, had met and been hurt by many well meaning people who made her aware that they tolerated her with Christian forbearance. She responded tonight to the casual way Marjorie accepted her.

"When is your birthday, Anugra?" Marjorie asked.

Anugra smiled shyly. "I do not know."

"Tell my wife your interesting life story, Anugra Bai," Robert urged. "She has never heard it."

"Brown Sahib, the father of Charis Missahib, found me in the jungle in the year of the big famine. I had been abandoned by my parents. No doubt they had deserted me deliberately in the forest, feeling a swift death from a wild beast was more merciful for me than one by slow starvation. Perhaps my parents had boys. I do not know, but in famine times if only some mouths can be fed, a good Hindu must choose his sons. I often wonder how my mother felt, or if she were already dead. At any rate, Brown Sahib heard me crying. The men with him insisted it was some animal. But his father's heart dictated otherwise. He turned from the path and found me in a clearing eating grass. How I survived being devoured by the wild beasts is a miracle. Perhaps I was not worth swallowing. I was little more than a skeleton. They kept me alive with milk dropped from an eyedropper.

"For days they did not name me. It scarcely seemed worthwhile. But Brown Memsahib never gave up. Her love and constant care accomplished the feat of restoring me to life. Charis was not yet born. Since the Brown Memsahib's first name was Grace, they had decided — if their expected baby were a girl — to name her Charis for her mother. Dr. Brown was a great scholar of languages, and loved especially the Greek. When it was evident that I would live, half in jest, he called me the Indian name for Grace, Anugra. He wanted, he said, to be surrounded by the Three Graces, Grace, Charis and Anugra."

"I never knew that you grew up in the mission."

"Actually, I didn't. Brown Memsahib did not long survive the birth of her child, and the Sahib took his baby daughter with him to America for a few years. I was four at the time. Sahib told me later it was a big decision for him to make. He wanted to take me, too, for he had always felt I was another daughter. But he knew too that heartache could follow my legal adoption into a white family." She underlined the word white with her voice. "It could mean that I would belong to neither race. He had seen it happen to other missionary friends who had taken orphaned children as their own. And so, not without personal grief, he arranged for my adoption by the pastor and wife who were then serving at Surrak Annund. I can still remember his tears at losing as he said 'two Graces.'

"I always made my home with my foster parents. When Brown Sahib decided to resume his missionary work alone, and brought his baby girl back with him, Charis and I became good friends. And in a special way, the Brown Sahib was my *ma-bap,* both mother and father. I think he was wise in his relationship to me, as he was in many things. I have always felt myself an Indian. He made me proud of my race. If my whole life had been spent in a white world, I wonder sometimes how I would feel. Charis has always been a dear younger sister to me. And yet, I like to live my own life in my own native way. I have a room in a house with my older foster brother and his wife."

"Did you know that Anugra Bai's brother is our pastor, Biswas?" Robert asked his wife. "He took over the work his father carried on so faithfully until his death."

Marjorie had not known. It seemed strange to her to see how much a woman of two worlds Anugra was. She spoke English with no accent. She was certainly at ease in their dining room. Marjorie tried to visualize her in the modest home of the village pastor. It seemed fantastic that she could be equally at home and content in one small room of the mud hut. She did not doubt she spoke the truth, for there was an aura of content that surrounded the girl, and it was catching.

Brown Sahib, thought Robert when Anugra finished her story, *was very wise in his training of Anugra. How strange, and how sad, that he was not able to give the same gift of contentment to the other Grace.*

When the finger bowls were brought to the table, Dhunwa had added a final touch of splendor by dropping flower petals in the water. It was kind of him. No doubt it was a gesture of penitence for his overbearing "I told you so's" of the morning. Marjorie had not failed to notice the butter carved like a lion and the other more common Dhunwa touches — all peace offerings no doubt — but this time he was really saying it with flowers. Just the same there was no cake, and they had been served rice pudding for dessert!

CHAPTER 23

CHARIS HAD BEEN GONE A WEEK when her post card addressed to the Townsends arrived from Agra. Marjorie read it. The message had been brief. "I feel already no further need for a vacation. I can gladly prescribe Dr. Glendenning for anything at anytime to anyone."

While Marjorie was still reading the day's mail, a messenger came into the compound. Recognizing the livery of the Rajah Sahib's servants, Marjorie left her desk on the veranda to meet him. She took the note from the tray upon which the messenger carried it. It was written in English, and it was a formally worded invitation to her from the Rajah himself asking her to come if at all possible to the palace that day.

She wrote her acceptance, and hastily changed into the blue gold-trimmed sari she had become accustomed to wearing for her palace visits. She compromised to old fashioned European standards by draping the end of the sari about her shoulders, and placing her pith helmet on her head. It had become stylish and safe for Europeans to go without this protection from the sun, and colored sunglasses seemed to afford sufficient safety from sunstroke for the majority. But her own extreme blondness had made Robert insist that she stay with the outmoded headgear.

She disliked wearing the ugly hat, but she had discovered that Robert, the doctor, was no man to cross. And so she jammed it over her soft page boy curls and started for the palace.

Instead of being ushered into the women's quarters, to her surprise, she was taken instead into the Rajah's study. The room was completely European, its furniture sturdy and although made from teak, lacking the ornateness of the hand carved and inlaid work which filled the other rooms. The only touch of the Orient was the large mounted tiger skin which hung full length on the wall behind the Rajah's desk.

The Rajah rose and extended his hand as she entered. Marjorie had not known that he had returned from his tour of his lands. She became worried by the expression on his face.

"Nothing is wrong with the Rani?" it prompted her to ask while shaking his hand.

He smiled affectionately at her when he heard the concern in her voice. "She is well. But there is something wrong. You have been a good teacher and a warm friend to my wife. That is why I turn to you for help."

Marjorie sat back and waited for the Rajah to continue.

"My wife," his voice was flat, "is insisting that I take her cousin for a second wife, since we are childless."

"Sundri!"

"You are surprised?"

"It doesn't seem that loving you as devotedly as she does, she would care to share you with another."

"If you felt that your husband's eternal destiny depended on a son, would you begrudge him a second wife when you could not fulfill the role of motherhood?"

"I don't believe I could share Robert with anyone," she found herself answering to her own surprise.

The Rajah's eyes twinkled. "You mean you would deny him heaven?"

She smiled. "Let us just say, Rajah Sahib, that I would deny him hell on this earth!"

The king chuckled. "I am of your same opinion, Memsahib-ji. That is why I come to you for help. I am distressed by my new Sundri, who spends all her time concentrating on my eternal destiny. I wish to resolve the situation, so that she can resume devoting all her time to my earthly comforts."

"You do not want a second wife?"

"No." He was emphatic.

"You would deny yourself heaven for your wife?"

The Rajah did not reply.

"You are not really a Hindu, are you, Rajah Sahib?"

"Now you, too, are becoming concerned with my eternal destiny. All I want is a little concern for my present state."

She ignored his teasing. "It is impossible for a woman to be happy in this life when she fears hell in the next for someone she loves — or for someone she admires." Her blue eyes challenged his.

"And so you are in league with my wife?"

"In my concern, yes. In my solution, no." She took from her bag a tract, the identical one she had handed to the holy man. As she handed it to him, the post card from Charis fell to the floor between them. He stooped to pick it up. Marjorie could not help but notice how European he was in every respect. Hindu etiquette would have made this menial task fall to her. As she took the card from him, she remembered the short message from Charis, and her face brightened.

"Rajah Sahib. Would your wife consent to an examination from a woman doctor?" She went on to describe the reputation and affection with which Dr. Glendenning was held. She mentioned especially the success with sterility cases the doctor had achieved. She knew she had his complete attention.

"Would she come?" he asked.

"My husband has arranged already for her to come to Surrak Annund to attend me. He will be happy to arrange a private palace appointment for Sundri Rani at that time."

"Have him do so, please. I shall insist that Sundri keep the date. It will be a compromise solution. Thank you. Thank you very much."

"And the cousin?"

"The cousin — but come and see what you have saved me from!"

Marjorie went with him to the women's quarters. Her curiosity was aroused to see the type of wife Sundri would suggest to her husband. When the girl was presented to her in the women's quarters, she could scarcely suppress a smile. Sundri Rani was obviously taking no chances on a rival. The woman might become a mother of sons, but she presented no other great threat. And she could understand better the Rajah's lack of interest in insuring his eternal destiny.

CHAPTER 24

CHARIS HERSELF ARRIVED AT THE bungalow only a short time after her post card. But Marjorie had already gone to the palace. It was to Robert that she broke her tragic news.

"I seem to bring disaster on all about me."

"Charis!" His voice was sharp.

"I am cured, Robert. I will never again attempt my own life. I can promise you that. But I have lost all desire to live." She had left and shut herself in her room.

There was nothing he could say or do. And he had been so absorbed in his worry over how this new experienced horror was going to affect Charis' delicate balance of mind, that he was quite unprepared for his own wife's reaction.

"I can't stay here. Not another day, Robert. Let me go home to America. I must go." She had shouted at him. And then she had begun to shake. "I'm scared. I'm yellow — clear through. I was afraid to save the *chowkidar*. I'm afraid now of the people. They murder and kill for three dollars. Why stay here any longer? Please, please let's go back home."

"Don't lose all sense of perspective, Marjorie. Stop thinking of the murderer for a moment. What about the trainman and all the others who tried to save Dr. Glendenning?"

"What about them? They could not keep her alive."

In the end he had given her a sedative. *How like Marjorie to react this way,* he thought. *Her fear again turns inward to herself. The great tragedy, the incomparable loss of a life like Dr. Glendenning's, has not even occurred to her.* Every time he seemed to feel any warmth growing between his estranged wife and himself, any hope for the future, some action of hers prompted by the same stupid self-interest chilled him to the bone.

The death of Dr. Glendenning had many unexpected repercussions. Dr. Townsend now had to divide his time between the two hospitals. He would stay two weeks at the mission hospital in Burrapur, trying to help the stricken staff there, and two weeks at his own hospital. He felt he was doing neither job well.

Marjorie, still not over the terror into which the news had plunged her, and left alone now many nights, had given in to Robert's advice. The *ayah* they had decided to hire for the new baby was asked to assume her duties earlier, and sleep in the Memsahib's bedroom at night. Marjorie was scarcely better than a child herself, and needed a nurse, Robert thought. And so Poulmani became a part of the mission circle.

Charis, after the first day of seclusion in her room, opened the door and coming out quietly, resumed her usual dutiful rounds. But Robert noticed all her usual warmth was gone. She had turned into a very efficient human robot. It was as if her heart still lived behind closed doors.

Not the least of the changes occurred in the palace of Surrak Annund. Dr. Glendenning's untimely death caused the Rajah reluctantly to capitulate. He had taken a second wife.

The cousin, to the discomfort of both Sundri Rani and Marjorie, was now a member of the English class. The Rajah insisted that this courtesy be extended to this new member of his harem. As a result, any further personal conversation with the Rani was impossible.

Marjorie felt handicapped by the presence of the new woman. This new wife was placid and dull. She made no effort to learn, but dutifully sat on her cushion in a corner chewing betel nut and pan leaves much like a contented cow chewing its cud. Rajkumari was more sallow in complexion than her cousin. She was short and stocky. She seemed to have no redeeming virtues at all.

Although they had no chance for private conversation, Marjorie could sense the strain already developing between the women. The very placidity of the new wife, who seemed impervious to any insults Sundri Rani in her flares of jealousy sent her way, made the Rani more hostile than ever. If the new wife did succeed in bearing the Rajah a son, Marjorie could not help but feel the delicate situation would only be made worse. Already Sundri seemed to have forgotten it was at her insistence that this new wife had been taken. The Rajah's sense of fair play displayed whenever he was called upon to give judgment

SONG BY THE RIVER 101

in household crises had not been anticipated by his young wife. She was displeased by the impartiality of his mind and was beginning to fear it indicated an equal impartiality of heart.

How the Rajah himself felt Marjorie had no way of knowing. He was no longer at the palace when she made her routine visits. No doubt he deliberately avoided her.

Marjorie felt a twinge of sympathy for the new wife; but Rajkumari's disposition discouraged any warmer feelings. On the other hand the domineering way in which the Rani treated the new bride displeased her. In this new mood of strain, and with little joy, she continued dutifully with the English lessons.

The Chinese, with their usual shrewdness, thought Marjorie, *well indicated with their hieroglyphic language the word "trouble" by a sketch of two women under one roof.* The palace, it seemed, was always now in a troubled state.

This same Chinese symbol for trouble, however, was present to a lesser degree in the mission bungalow.

On her return Charis kept as much as possible to herself. Still acutely conscious of her dead friend's criticism — perhaps more so because her death had underlined her principles so vividly — she avoided any unnecessary contact with Robert. She would have liked to develop a friendship with his wife, but found little in Marjorie to attract her. She knew why. Her own basic common sense made her realize that Dr. Glendenning had been laboring with her only the principles which she felt were pertinent for her. The doctor, she knew, was not oblivious to the millstones that many missionary wives were about their husbands' necks.

And Marjorie is one, she thought candidly. *I resent her because of it. And I can only hope and pray that this constant drag at Robert to give up his life work will be of no avail. Marjorie,* she thought analytically, *has spent her life developing only one side of herself. She has done this well. She is always attractive and well groomed. Even now, she carries herself with an effortless grace that is almost Indian. Marjorie is also an intelligent woman. But she has been content to use her brain only to develop a witty, superficial brilliance. She chatters well. Still it is impossible to dismiss Marjorie's personality as fluff. The cuteness is only a facade which sheathes a mind that is clever to achieve its own ends. It is Marjorie's soul which disturbs me most. I can never contact it. It is impossible to speak of any* spiritual topic with her without the conversation detouring into the customary dead end of trivialities. This is the big barrier across any deep friendship between us.

Should I make more effort to reach her? Would she resent my approaches? In the end, Charis, from sheer lack of drive, permitted the situation to slide along. And so, although Robert's prolonged absences threw the two women together more for companionship, she realized that actually the two scarcely ever met on the only plane which mattered to her.

Marjorie, for her part, disliked Charis. She was frank about it to herself. *I admire her integrity, her industry, but in the end so much display of goodness wearies me. I suppose it shows a lack of a finer spirit in me, or maybe I am just like Sundri Rani at heart — a cat with claws. If Robert were not so observant of the good qualities of Charis, perhaps I would then be more aware of them.* She made no overtures toward friendship and felt no regrets. It was a cold peace.

A new influence came into Marjorie's life with the entrance of the *ayah*, Poulmani, into the group of domestics who occupied much of her time. Marjorie enjoyed calling the little woman Flower, which was the English translation of her name. Poulmani was a Christian convert from the lowest caste. Many from this depressed group, with nothing to lose, swarmed into the church at the turn of the century, and became, in spite of efforts to sift their sincerity, "rice Christians." Who with an empty stomach would not accept a new god for a bowlful of rice? And now the Christian church in India faced what the church at home had faced for generations — the problem of evangelizing its own membership.

But Poulmani was truly a flower springing up from among this clump of weeds. She was not only from this low caste, she also was unfortunate enough to be in the sad category of an Indian widow. The transforming news that Jesus loved even her, a sweeper and a widow, filled her whole life with glory. She, who had been abused since she had been widowed at the age of eight, had God's Holy Word read to her indicating His concern for the widowed. She wept openly when she understood the words. She who formerly scarcely felt she could call herself a member of the human race could now claim to be a child of God. She embodied in her life the challenge of the hymn, "Love so amazing, so divine, demands my life, my soul, my all."

Robert's choice for an *ayah* had been wise. A new enveloping love stole into the bungalow with her quiet presence. She walked about on her tiny bare feet, making no sound on the cement floor of the bedroom, attending eagerly to the comforts of her new mistress. Her face became radiant whenever the coming of the new baby was mentioned. It was as if she felt the expected child were her very own. Her empty arms would be full at last.

Marjorie enjoyed the attentions the *ayah* showed her. She never stirred at night, but the woman, who slept native fashion on a mat by the door, responded with a whisper. *She never sleeps,* thought Marjorie, *she is like my own mother.* She could not help but smile to think of how her sophisticated mother would enjoy comparison with a sweeper woman. And although Marjorie's fear of the natives did not disappear, the sight of the woman's body across her threshold, a living door, kept some of the terrors back.

CHAPTER 25

ROBERT, MAN FASHION, while relieved that the women seemed to be doing so well in his absence, felt a twinge of regret that he was so little missed.

He doggedly stirred up the dust between the two stations, and felt at times that he was carrying two worlds on his back. The approaching day of Independence for India failed to loom as big as it had done in his mind prior to his newly added duties, and so he scarcely gave a second thought to the fact that on that fatal day he would be on the staff of the hospital in Burrapur.

He was in the operating room when the first horrifying news began to trickle in. Rumors of murder, pillage, atrocities flew thick and fast. Finally a British railroad official came rushing in, confirming the worst, to ask his help. Five miles outside the city station the train had been ambushed by an enraged Hindu mob and hundreds of Mohammedans had been butchered.

Robert grabbed his medical bag and drove with the man to the scene. More than half the casualties were beyond his aid. The bodies had not only been stabbed but hacked to bits. One small body had been totally dismembered. The British official stumbled over the disemboweled body of a pregnant woman, and staggered over to the ditch. Robert wished he, too, could give in to the overwhelming nausea which arose in him; but grimly he carried on. Stretchers were improvised, and as many cases as possible were started on their way to the mission hospital.

Robert was glad the women were in Surrak Annund, away from the big city where large mingled populations of Hindus and Mohammedans bore this horrible fruitage of centuries of distrust. It was only later in the day, when news began to come in that this massacre was not confined to the railroad centers, but that all of India seemed to have gone mad, that he began to worry over the safety of those left in Surrak Annund. He gave emergency instructions to the staff, and over their urgent protest and concern for his safety, he raced the jeep back over the jungle roads, horrified by what he might find in his own home.

Marjorie awakened at the loud insistent coughing at her screen door. It was the polite equivalent to a pounding on the door. She looked around for Poulmani, but her pallet was empty. Uneasy, she slipped into her robe and slippers and called, "Quoi hai?" (Who's there?)

A voice from the darkness answered her, "I come from the hospital, Memsahib-ji. There is grave trouble in the village. Missahib Charis sent me for you."

"What is the trouble?"

"Memsahib-ji, you must hurry. It is *Swa-raj*." He did not wait any longer and disappeared into the darkness.

Swa-raj, independence, why should it concern her? But Charis was not one to be easily alarmed. She had better go. Marjorie putting her thoughts into action started for the closet to get a dress, when Poulmani came in from the duftar. She was carrying the three guns the mission possessed and a heavy box of cartridges.

"There is not time to dress, Memsahib-ji. Quick, carry your clothes with you. We must not be found here. The whole village has gone mad. At first the men were fighting only men, but now they kill any who cross their path." She grabbed her mistress by the arm and pushed her urgently out the door. "Here, take this. Is it loaded?"

Marjorie took the gun, checked it and nodded. Following the woman who seemed to be able to see in the dark, Marjorie stumbled down the path behind her. She could hear screams and shooting and savage yells from beyond the rice fields.

Charis was waiting anxiously for them at the door of the hospital when they arrived. Already a barricade of sorts had been placed about the large veranda, and the patients had been moved into the halls.

"Thank God you brought the guns." She took the ammunition from Poulmani, handed one rifle to Anugra, and kept the other for herself. Marjorie still held the gun which the *ayah* had placed in her hands.

"I want you to stand watch by this window, Marjorie. The moment anyone crosses that veranda barricade, shoot, and shoot to kill."

"To kill! Charis, are you out of your mind?"

"You can shoot, can't you?"

"Yes, but not at a human being."

"If any of those looters break loose here, you need have no scruples. Believe me, you won't be shooting at a human being."

"I thought you were a Christian," said Marjorie indignantly.

Charis turned angrily to her. "This is no time for a discussion on the principles of pacifism. Let me just say this. If I went berserk in the hospital and tried to kill the patients, the Christian thing to do would be to kill me. It would be not only the kindest thing you could do for the patients," she said grimly, "but also to me. You would be saving me from myself."

At that moment a bloodcurdling yell came from the peepul tree in the yard. Marjorie blanched. "The Saddhu! We have forgotten the Saddhu!"

"Cover me," said Charis, and opened the door. But when Marjorie hesitated, cowering behind the open door, Anugra stepped forward, and stood in the doorway like an avenging angel in her white nurse's uniform with a modern sword, a gun. She shot repeatedly in the air as Charis half crawled, half crept to the peepul tree.

The firing stopped and Marjorie heard the sound of a body being dragged across the porch and through the doorway. She bolted the door after the women, and looked down at her feet where the Saddhu lay. The poor man's side had been slashed open, and blood gushed out and mingled with the gray ashes and saffron that stained his body. *His eyes,* thought Marjorie, *his eyes are still alive.*

Charis took time only to superficially bandage the wound. Then she and Anugra half carried, half dragged the man to a pallet in the corner. The other terrified patients were not happy to have him.

"Missahib-ji," one bolder one protested, "if they know you have the holy man here it will endanger all of our lives. He is half dead already. Throw him out."

"For shame," she replied. "You a Hindu to turn on your own."

"They are coming," shouted another patient in panic.

"Quiet!" she ordered. Even from their pallets on the floor through the reflections in the windows they could see the flickering torches of the approaching mob. Charis deliberately unbolted the door. "Bolt it after me," she called back over her shoulder. But no one obeyed.

They heard her voice clearly through the door. "Halt! Or I'll shoot!"

They could see nothing, but they heard an angry threatening voice reply, "Step aside, Missahib-ji. We do not want to harm you. But we want you to send out to us every Hindu patient that you have. You may keep the Christians. We will not harm them."

A groan went up from the huddled patients.

"You know better than that, Husan." Charis called the ringleader by name. "Did I ask you your faith when I gave you back your son from the arms of death?"

"We are at war now."

"War, Husan, does not change eternal principles. This is a Christian hospital. We operate on Christian principles. We do not ask any who come to us, 'Are you Hindu, Mohammedan, or even are you a Christian?' We ask only one question, 'Are you sick?' And if any are sick, in Christ's name we give aid. Is it fair for you to ask me to deny to others the same help that I have given gladly to you?"

She is magnificent, thought Marjorie. *But will she win?*

The crowd of torches came closer to the windows. One angry voice shouted, "Kill them! Kill them all!"

"Kill me first!" Her voice challenged.

"Silence!" Husan thundered. "No one will cross that barricade. That is an order. Back to the village!"

The windows became gradually darker as the torches receded. It was only when the invaders had given the yard back to the night, and it was dark again, that Charis stepped back in. One patient crawled painfully across the floor and pressed his face against the sole of Charis' shoe. A Hindu, to whom a woman was next to nothing, to whom shoe leather meant defilement, was paying a brave woman his highest tribute.

The Saddhu lay and looked.

CHAPTER 26

WHEN ROBERT RETURNED TO Surrak Annund the women were still in the emergency fort, the hospital. No further attempt had been made to storm their sanctuary; but while rumors were still flying about atrocities practiced by both sides in this spontaneous revolution, it seemed wisest to huddle there together.

He had driven the jeep to the doors of the bungalow, and raced madly through the deserted building, fearing with each door he opened what he might find. But there was nothing to be seen, not even any sign of pillage. When he had at last found the women safe and unharmed in the hospital waiting room, only his eyes betrayed the horrors he had imagined.

"Did you have any trouble here?" he asked.

"We had a minor scare," said Charis calmly.

Anugra looked at Marjorie as if expecting her to relate the heroism of the night. *I'm not big enough,* thought Marjorie, *to contradict Charis, to tell the true story and build her up any higher in his eyes. If she wants to dismiss it so summarily, so be it.*

"We would all be dead," said Anugra, as her eyes rebuked the Memsahib, "if it were not for the Missahib's bravery."

Robert listened in silence to the story. *The very absence of my name will indicate the lack of role I played in the event,* thought Marjorie bitterly, and did not wait for the end.

Robert came to find her in the hospital room which she now shared with Poulmani. There was no rebuke, however, either in his manner or his words. All he said was, "If you still want to go to the States to have the baby, Marjorie, I will take you."

It was her moment of triumph. But she could not find any happiness in it. "Thank you, Robert," was all she said.

Charis met Robert in the hall outside his wife's room. "I

have just told Marjorie we will go to the States for the birth of the child.

"Don't look like that, Charis." He pleaded when he saw her face. "I am not deserting my work. I am not just pampering my wife. I have steadfastly refused to leave this country. But the situation has changed. Too much has happened. As a doctor I feel now that the trip home is indicated. Marjorie needs mentally a sense of security at this time which I cannot give her — not here at least."

"Will you come back, Robert?"

"Of course," he said brusquely, but a frown crossed his face at the question.

Charis remained motionless while Robert walked away. Then impulsively she swung open the door to his wife's room.

"May I speak to you a moment, Marjorie?"

Marjorie looked up wearily. "Sit down." She continued to lie propped up in her hospital bed.

"Robert has just told me you are going to the States for the birth of your baby." Her voice showed her effort at self control. "He expects to come back to the field, you know?"

"Yes, I know." Marjorie's words were a challenge.

"I am here to ask one question. Will he?"

"Do you expect an answer?"

"Yes."

"Well then, here is your answer." Marjorie articulated each word deliberately. "He will not come back if I can help it."

Charis let out her breath in a sigh. "Do you realize what your plans will do to Robert — if you succeed?"

"Do you realize what it will mean to me, if I don't?" Marjorie spoke with feeling. "I hate this filthy land of yours. You have been inoculated from childhood against its sights, its stench, its death. All you can see is the beauty of the champa blossoms."

"You chose his land when you chose Robert."

"Charis, do you love Robert?"

Charis did not drop her eyes. "Let us say I did love him. Did you ever know, Marjorie, why I went to the hills? I tried to take my own life. I know now why I did. I loved Robert; and I knew my love was a sin. I thought I could not stop loving him as long as I lived."

"You, Charis. You attempted suicide!"

"Yes," she answered calmly. "I want you to know that although I once loved your husband, I no longer do. I have overcome my love. It hasn't been done in a day." Her voice trembled. "But I have discovered it isn't necessary to stop breathing to stop loving. Any love to survive must be fed and nurtured and I have learned to discipline my thoughts away from him, to starve my love to death. Please believe me, Marjorie, I did not realize my own feelings at the time. I allowed myself to slip into the situation. The moment I made myself face my heart, I started to fight for my integrity; and I have won.

"And so I am speaking to you, from my love of humanity, and not my love for Robert, don't take him from his work. Go home if you must and have your child, but come back, please come back."

Marjorie heard the starch rustle of the uniform as Charis left the bedroom. *It was a great and generous gesture,* she thought. *Charis humiliated herself for Robert's sake. It must have taken tremendous heart to do it. But I can't rally to the gesture, for unfortunately, I am not a great and generous person. I want my baby, I want Robert, and I want America.*

CHAPTER 27

ONLY GRADUALLY DID THE TOTAL picture of Independence Day in India reach the Surrak Annund outpost. For even though the overland mail runner never missed a day, the news in the Indian newspaper was strictly censored. Only in time did the Townsends learn that an official estimate placed the loss of Moslem lives in New Delhi, the capital city of the new India, at one thousand. And one civil official in that city indicated that no accurate count was possible amid the confusion, murder, arson and looting which lasted almost a week. He thought ten thousand dead would be a fairer estimate. And that was in one Indian city.

From across the border of the new State of Pakistan news was equally serious. One American news commentator said it was the bloodiest revolution known in the history of man. It was made much worse than any other because it was totally unplanned. It was a spontaneous combustion fanned and kept ablaze by rumors of atrocity and counteratrocity, until in the end the blame was equally divided.

From all this morass of blood one fact slowly emerged: Christians had been spared. In New Delhi they wore big red cloth crosses across their chests. And homes in many areas, smeared with the sign of the cross, were not even looted. Enraged Mohammedans cleverly employed the ruse of checking on genuine Christians by asking any whose faith they questioned to recite the Lord's Prayer or the Ten Commandments. Woe be to any Christian who had neglected to memorize these Scriptures. Wherever Christian blood had been shed, it had been shed in error. The experience through which the Surrak Annund hospital passed was typical of the treatment accorded all the missions.

Both Hindus and Moslems agreed they needed the Christian Church in their hour of crisis. And as their foundations were shaken to the roots, and they fell on each other with any weapons at hand — hockey sticks, clubs, knives — and where no weapon was available, when with their own hands and nails they bit and tore each other apart, the sick and wounded on both sides crawled when it was physically possible, to the nearest mission for sanctuary.

One of the greatest tragedies in the Surrak Annund area was the murder of the beloved Rajah of the district. On the night of the great massacre he had been in the northernmost tip of his kingdom. There his own *jat* — people — had been the offenders. In one small village where people of both faiths had lived together in peace for generations, supreme madness took control and the victors built a living bonfire in the village square. Alive and screaming with fear and pain, unfortunate victims were fed into the flames like so much fuel. When tiny children crawled feebly out they were clubbed back to roast alive.

Sick with horror at the massacre, the Rajah had arrived and bravely but foolishly had tried to stop the maddened berserk crowd. And they, who in calmer times loved him, had turned on him like mad dogs and clubbed him to the ground. He had lingered between life and death a few days, but before the palanquin bearing his body arrived back at his palace he was dead.

All night long in Surrak Annund, since the Partition, the burning ghats where the Hindus cremated their dead had been aglow, and none at the mission had realized that one of the new burning bodies had been that of their friend, the Rajah. They heard the news the day following the cremation, when the palace bearer came with a note summoning Marjorie to the palace. Robert was anxious and did not want her to go. He capitulated, finally, only on the condition that he drive her there in the jeep; and while she entered the courtyard, he stood guard outside the palace gates.

Marjorie was shocked at the appearance of the Rani. Her lovely hair was all gone, for her head had been shaved close to the scalp with a sharp razor. She lay moaning and beating her head against the floor, and wailing the Hindu widow's chant, "Oh my beloved, why hast thou left me? Have I not always been a virtuous wife? Have I not always strived to please

SONG BY THE RIVER

thee? Have I not always fed thee the foods thou lovest, seasoned with garlic, turmeric, mustard and spices?" In her customary corner, as phlegmatic as ever sat the second wife. There was no flicker of emotion on her face.

The servant girl entered to announce the arrival of the village priest. The Rani straightened herself with an effort. Her face lightened for a moment when she saw Marjorie, and holding tight to her hand she walked out with her into the sunlight for the first time unveiled. Marjorie sat as inconspicuously as possible in a wicker chair, one full of memories of happier visits, and watched while her friend fulfilled the required customs.

The Rani fell flat on her face and started to inch her way on her stomach across the veranda to where the priest squatted. His face was a painted mask of ashes and saffron; but unlike the Saddhu in the mission compound, it seemed to Marjorie that his large bold eyes were wholly evil. When she reached his feet, the queen took from the pouch which hung at her waist a pill and proffered it to the priest. He refused to touch it. As Marjorie listened her disgust mounted, for it became evident what the pill ingredients were. They were pulverized parts of the Rajah's own body, and the Rani was seeking his salvation by urging the priest to swallow the gruesome capsule. The priest disdained her request, but it was soon evident that he was holding out for a better price. From a basket a servant brought, the queen took a handful of gems and slowly let them trickle through her fingers at the priest's feet. Many of the jewels Marjorie recognized as having been Sundri's favorite ornaments. No price was too great to pay by the bereaved widow for her beloved's salvation. But still the priest remained adamant. Finally when an elephant was offered in addition to the piles of gold and gems which he had already secured, he nodded his consent, and solemnly in the presence of all swallowed the pill.

It was the first time many of the people had seen the face of their Rani. Now as a widow she had no longer the right of privacy, to hide behind her veil. They stared curiously. And Marjorie could feel for her friend as she suffered what was to her this final indignity. When her part in this interchange was concluded, in spite of her inner torment, with a pathetic dignity the Rani walked back into the palace. Marjorie rose and quietly followed her. When they reached the sanctuary of the *zenana* the little Rani began again to beat her breast and wail. Marjorie sat down on the floor beside her distraught friend and wept with her quietly without a sound. Rajkumari sat stolidly by, and watched the two weeping women with a tearless face. Her very silence spoke so loudly that Sundri became suddenly aware of her presence.

"Rajkumari is with child," the Rani spoke at last directly to her friend. The inflection in her voice as much as her words indicated her change of attitude toward her former rival. Rajkumari's days of servitude were ended. In an unsettled India she would now be a cherished vessel for she would provide an heir for the Rajah; but what was more important to the Rani, the second wife would be now a carefully tended vehicle by which the Rajah's eternal bliss would be secured. He had lived a blameless life, she reasoned, and if she could insure this necessary merit for him, the gods might even be good enough to permit him to escape from the endless wheel of life. "He may never need to live in another incarnation," she confided to her friend, "but with Rajkumari's help he may escape into the blessedness of *Nirvana*."

As she spoke, Marjorie noticed the Rani fingering a big bag tied about her throat. Seeing her glance, the queen said, "When the Rajah, my husband, was cremated yesterday, we threw *dhotis* and *pugrees*, the most splendid we could buy, on the flames, that if my husband must live again he will not be in want for suitable clothing. But I am hoping he may not need them. In this bag are some of his ashes. I crawled myself about the ash heap after his body had been consumed and the ashes had cooled. A part of his body is here." She gestured to the bag. "You saw the priest swallow some. These," she touched the gruesome neck piece, "I shall take on a pilgrimage to the Ganges River, and sprinkle them there on the holy river. Thus I shall do everything in my power to insure his salvation."

"Do you think Rajah Sahib would have wanted you to do this, Sundri Rani?" Marjorie could not help but ask.

The Rani flushed. "You must not even suggest to me that he would not. I could not bear to think he was not a good Hindu, not now. Please, please do not even in your mind damn him to the wheel of life again."

Marjorie was upset, sick and ill at all she had seen and heard. It seemed obvious there was little more she could do at this time. Gravely she enfolded the little queen in her arms, and in the native fashion kissed her first on one wet cheek and then the other. She had left the women's quarters before she realized she had forgotten to say farewell to the second wife. But she had no desire to return.

Her own child stirred restlessly within her. She scarcely noticed the tiny flutter. For simultaneously there stirred within her, with the beating, too, of tiny wings, a quickening, a fluttering faith. It seemed that the horror of the sights she had seen, raw heathendom at work in the heart of a friend, had accomplished what a sheltered lifetime had never done.

The old Marjorie stayed behind in the palace courtyard, and a new Marjorie emerged, a new Marjorie in that moment was quickened. And as she passed the phallic symbol which stood beside the courtyard temple, she shuddered to think her lovely friend would be doing obeisance with renewed zeal to this emblem of fertility. She prayed, for the first time, for the salvation of her friend.

CHAPTER 28

As THE JEEP SQUEEZED ITS WAY down the wider village streets which twined and choked about the palace, the Townsends noticed evidence of the looting of the past days. There were broken store windows, gutted mud houses, burnt thatch roofs, and even bloodstained dust still on the streets. But already in a land where death wears a familiar face, life was resuming. The appearance of the jeep — even today — brought out its usual crowd of happy children. Their little naked bodies, except in the cases of the high born who wore the sacred beads — and nothing but this string of beads — formed as it were the tail of a kite.

These children, from them perhaps a new village will emerge, a new, a better Surrak Annund, Robert thought. *What potentialities for good or evil incubate in these little laughing children. God grant the mission can reach them.*

As the jeep reached the open *midan* which they must cross before they reached the bungalow, Robert stepped gradually, carefully on the gas, accelerating slowly until finally even the hardiest yelled his farewell and let go.

Marjorie had scarcely spoken since she left the palace, and Robert was uneasy at the whiteness of her face. But he did not press any conversation upon her which she evidently did not wish to initiate.

There still had been no word from the airlines office. Air was the only possible way for them to reach the States now, with any degree of safety. As it was, Robert was apprehensive of the train journey to Calcutta. The slow bumpy jeep ride to Burrapur would have to be taken in easy stages. These days even he was beginning to watch for the overland mail.

In the end *Swa-raj* played a role also in the domestic situation of the Townsends. Due to the large exodus of the European population of India, now that the new government was in power, every available plane seat was taken for months ahead. Marjorie was apathetic when she learned there was now no escape from Surrak Annund. Ironically, it was Robert who was most disturbed by the bad news.

The days that followed Partition were hard ones for Robert, and for the villages which Robert considered his parish. The hordes of people made homeless by the days of terror were swollen in number by an unending stream of refugees who poured out of the new State of Pakistan. These people propped up shacks, using the walls of any gutted building that was left standing, and with sticks and skins they built their makeshift shelters. The first breath of wind would collapse these pitiful homes.

Some of the newcomers huddled together in tents on the *midan*, which had been turned into an emergency refugee camp. Robert made it a point to stop at the camp daily, for disease easily transmitted by the crowded masses was a grave and ever-present threat.

In some ways the starvation cases which Robert handled were more tragic even than those of mutilation. It was agony for him, and for the parents, to see especially the bodies of the little children become bloated with hunger. Their empty stomachs puffed up like balloons. Above this swelling the pathetic skeleton of ribs peeped through the wrinkled skin. In the sunken eyes that rolled in their deep sockets, the light of reason had already been extinguished. These little adults — for even the tiniest could hardly be called a child — scavenged about in the garbage dumps of the village, and fought with pariah dogs for the small amounts of food which the "haves" threw out of their doorways for the "have nots."

Robert remembered that someone once said, "The whole world could easily be fed from the garbage pails of America." Still he could feel no lingering resentment for his own people, when every week boxes of precious food and medicines came in. America, the profligate, was also America, the generous hearted. And as he and his helpers wrenched apart the containers of this manna from heaven, pride in his own country surged deep within as he saw the blocked letters, "U.S.A." But even more significant were the words, "Church World Service."

He distributed food and clothing, grateful for the agencies which made this largess possible. He was successful in a large measure because of these gifts to the masses to be able to persuade them to also accept the less welcome but equally necessary inoculations and vaccinations. And so in his district he was grateful that no epidemics broke out. But while the people stayed alive, they lived in conditions far below even the normal sub-normal life of the average Indian peasant.

In the hospital Robert tarried, whenever he could spare the time, with his unusual new patient, the Saddhu of the peepul tree. It was a miracle that the man was still alive. It was as if the little flicker of life he had seemed to possess was too small to merit the effort of snuffing it out.

Or as the Upanishads, whose teaching the Saddhu followed, stated, "The person, not larger than a thumb, the inner self, is always settled in the heart of man. Let a man draw that self forth from his body with steadiness, as one draws the pith from a reed. Let him know that self as the bright, as the immortal." It seemed as if the process of self-meditation, the drawing forth of this inner self had not ended for the holy man, and so he lived on in his own rarified atmosphere.

He had remained speechless for days, when one morning he had surprised Robert by asking him as he was dressing his wound, "Why do you do it?"

"Because you need it," the doctor replied, "and our Holy Book," he pointed to the Bible which was placed by his bedside, "tells us — let me read a story to you." He turned to the parable of the Good Samaritan and read it quietly to the man.

"A good Hindu," the Saddhu said, when the story had ended, "would have 'passed by on the other side.' All suffering is caused by sin. When you help a sufferer who is punished by the gods you risk the wrath of heaven yourself. We are taught not to interfere with a man's *kismet*."

"Our theology is alike, in that we both recognize the presence of sin, and we too feel that some suffering may be a direct fruit of sin and the wrath of God. We differ in this: We feel that all merit suffering, for all have sinned. If we all received what we deserved we would all be the most miserable of men. The fact that some seem more fortunate than others in this life does not mean that these deserve more than others this state of theirs. This is a sinful world. In this world the scales of justice are not equally balanced. Or to paraphrase one of our great theologians, Augustine, there is enough punishment in this world to indicate that there will be punishment in the next world. But not enough to make punishment in the next world unnecessary. We feel, therefore, that we must help all in need, for 'there but for the grace of God, go I.'"

"And what of the future? The Upanishads teach us that a *purusha* sits in the heart of man and controls his entire life. During a man's life this *purusha* can be seen through his eyes, especially the pupil. At a man's death it escapes through a small hole at the top of his skull and is reabsorbed into the great universal soul."

"In this we differ, too. Our idea of heaven is not a cessation of our own being. It is a continuation of our own selves in a new wondrously redeemed body. A Christian is taught to enjoy the good pleasures of this life and to anticipate still more the life to come."

"How may a man reach your heaven?"

Robert was sympathetic as he answered the man who had spent most of his life enduring self-inflicted torment to accumulate merit for his soul. He touched with compassion the withered arm as he spoke, "A Christian is taught not to let any of his body or personality wither from lack of use. He must use all his mind, heart and strength in the service of God. But even as he works he feels none of his service, however devoted it may be, can merit him heaven."

"Alas," said the holy man, "there is then no sure hope for you also."

"Ah! But there is!" Robert continued. "Man by his works cannot atone for sin. But our Holy Book tells us that God, the only one who could, did atone for us by sending His Son to die on the Cross for our sins." Deliberately he told the man, who heard it for the first time, the story of Jesus. He took him through Christ's incarnation to His death and resurrection; he led him from the crib to the cross and the crown.

The holy man wept. *How could any man worthy of the designation man fail to be moved by the tremendous story of redemption?* thought Robert.

Robert sat quietly by his bed. "You have given me much to meditate about. Let me think about this news," the Saddhu said.

As Robert left he took from his pocket a small leaflet. "Since you can read, I brought you a story of another holy man who sought the Truth even as you." He placed in the patient's hand the story of the convert to Christianity, Saddhu Sunder Singh.

God grant, he prayed silently, *this man may not only be touched, but turned about — converted.*

CHAPTER 29

THE SPIRIT OF GOD was at work not only in the hospital but in the bungalow, not only in the life of Robert's patient but in that of his wife.

Marjorie was restless. There was nowhere that she could be completely alone. She wanted a place where she could think uninterruptedly. In desperation she went into Robert's office. He would be at the refugee camp most of the day, and at least a measure of privacy would be secured. Idly she picked up a crumpled sheet of foolscap paper that had been stuck in a pigeonhole of the big desk. She smoothed out the sheets and there facing her were three badly drawn circles. It took only a cursory glance to reveal what they symbolized.

In the weeks and months that had elapsed since her night of revelation in the Indian hut, Marjorie had managed to push this unpleasant memory away. She had made it a policy to ignore any unpleasantness which touched her life in any way. She had almost convinced herself that she had misread Robert's face, and now in her new melted mood it was heartbreaking to meet this new and written revelation of the true mind of her husband.

"I could never have kept my husband if he had not been a Christian and faithful to his vows." The evidence was in her hands; she stared at the almost empty circle which represented her total personality. She grimaced. "This is what he sees when he looks at me."

She had meant to spend the time trying to inspect her own deep but as yet incoherent thoughts about God. Instead she was driven down earthward by this scrap of paper. Even a day ago, if she had been forced to think over her domestic problems, she would have felt secure in the power of her own personality to recapture Robert's wavering affection — had she really desired to work at it. Her personality! She looked at her husband's sketch again. Deliberately she took the circle and stood beside the mirror holding it beside her own pretty face. "This," she shook the paper, "is what he sees in me!" It was self-evident her husband remained bound to her by principle, by the rules of the Book, not by her magnetic attraction.

The *punkha* above her stopped in its pathway across the ceiling, and a cry, more a whimper than a cry, from the veranda, intercepted her thoughts.

"Never alone," muttered Marjorie as she went to the doorway. "Even now, I am interrupted!"

At first she saw only the strange position of Mohardas, the *punkha walla*. He had his knees drawn tightly to his thin chest. His eyes were fixed and glassy. Was he ill? Then she, too, saw and shared his terror. Edging the veranda were pots of Easter lilies. Around one of these something moved. It uncoiled itself and slid toward the terrified boy. In some way Mohardas' rhythmic thumping as he pulled the rope of the *punkha* had disturbed the cobra from its rest, and it was resentful and full of anger. She could never reach a gun in time. She watched hypnotically as the snake raised its head, puffed out its thick neck into a hood, and before her terrified eyes struck at the paralyzed *punkha walla*. It sank its poisonous fangs deep into his arm, then mission accomplished, with a swift and graceful glide disappeared behind the flowerpots and over the porch to where its hole must be.

"I must do something this time," Marjorie fumed at her own impotence, her own ignorance. The poison must be removed at once. That much she remembered. Charis was at the hospital. Marjorie knew there would not be time enough to wait for her arrival. She grabbed a pocket knife from Robert's desk drawer, and slashed a deep gash in the boy's arm directly over the marks of the fangs. Mohardas was too frightened to whimper. She buried her own lips against the brown skin, and deliberately sucked out the venom, spitting out each horrible mouthful of the bloody mixture to the porch with shuddering distaste. She was afraid to stop, and was still sucking the wound when help arrived. It was Charis who relieved her with her usual efficiency.

Marjorie gagged in the bathroom as she rinsed her mouth endlessly with warm water. But she felt pleased with herself.

This was at least one occasion when she had rallied to the crisis of the moment. Perhaps it was a good omen.

At dinner that evening she basked in the generous accounting that Charis gave of the incident, and in Robert's obvious pleasure in her deed, "That was a very generous action, Marjorie, to risk your life for his."

But as his words reached her she paled at their full implication. "Risked my life?"

The undisguised horror in her voice had caused Robert to reply tonelessly, "If you had had any open cut or abrasion in your mouth, or on your tongue, the venom would have been deadly to you."

"I never knew that," her voice trembled.

"That seems quite obvious." There was no expression in Robert's voice.

Marjorie flushed with a new sensitivity. "I wonder what I would have done if I had known."

No one answered. It was perhaps as well, for none of them — not even Marjorie — honestly felt she would have deliberately risked her own life for that of the little black boy. Marjorie felt a new emotion steal over her. She was ashamed.

CHAPTER 30

MARJORIE DREAMED THAT NIGHT of snakes, horrible crawling serpents that twined about her. She fought the crushing slimy bodies. She dodged repeatedly from the striking cobras, until in her exhaustion one struck through her guard. She felt its sharp death dealing sting. *I am dying*, she thought, *nothing can save me*.

Lips, cool lips were pressed against her wound. But when she looked, no one was there. In some way, peculiar to dreams, she knew that her invisible helper was endangering his own life by his action, and she struggled feebly to stop him. But he held her firm until all the poison was gone.

One by one the snakes slid away, and left her alone, alive! But not alone, for at her feet her rescuer lay dead. She stooped to turn over the now visible rescuer, to seek his face. She knew whose face she would see. She cried to know her fears confirmed. Her salvation had cost the life of the Son of God.

> He died that we might be forgiven,
> He died to make us good,
> That we might go at last to Heaven,
> Saved by His precious blood.

She was singing this song when she awakened.

The moment for her self examination could no longer be postponed. And Marjorie in the remaining night hours turned the light of the Scriptures, with which she had been familiar since a child, on her own life. A bombardment of relevant verses hit her. She opened her Bible to passage after passage that seemed written especially for her.

The Book of Romans had something for her on every page. In the twelfth chapter and the second verse she read, "For I say, through the grace given unto me, to every man that is among you, not to think of himself more highly than he ought to think." And again in the same chapter in the sixteenth verse was the line, "Be not wise in your own conceits."

Romans, the fourteenth chapter and the seventh verse, reminded her that "None of us liveth to himself." And in Romans, the fifteenth chapter, the second and third verses, she took to heart the exhortation, "Let every one of us please his neighbour for his good to edification. For even Christ pleased not himself."

She felt the rebuke of the verses in I Corinthians, as she read in the fourth chapter, the seventh verse, "For who maketh thee to differ from another? and what hast thou that thou didst not receive? now if thou didst receive it, why dost thou glory, as if thou hadst not received it." And again she winced as she read in the thirteenth chapter parts of the fourth and fifth verses, "Charity vaunteth not itself, is not puffed up . . . ."

In Philippians, the second chapter and the fourth verse, she found a verse which she read over and over again, "Look not every man on his own things, but every man also on the things of others."

The last verse she meditated upon was for her the strongest rebuke of all; it was Matthew, the sixteenth chapter and the twenty-fifth verse, "For whosoever will save his life shall lose it: and whosoever will lose his life for my sake shall find it."

Her prayer came at the dawn, and was the simple one of the publican, "God, be merciful to me, a sinner."

After Marjorie's conversion her main interest began to turn out away from herself for the first time in her life. And whereas formerly all her associations had been significant only as they related to her, she discovered now a new concern for others for their own sakes alone.

Since the Rani was away on her pilgrimage to the Ganges River her English classes at the palace had stopped. But her friend was often in her thoughts, and Marjorie longed to resume her easy relationship with the queen motivated as she was now with a new zeal for her friend's soul. It would be a difficult feat to win the Rani for Christ, even harder than when her more moderate husband had been alive. But she wanted to try. How sad that it was always so difficult to reach the high and mighty for God. It was so everywhere, not only in India; and in all times, not just the present. Even in Christ's own day in Palestine His own band, His stalwart few, had been chosen from the lowly.

In many ways Poulmani was more fortunate by birth than Sundri. Sundri, a queen, a Kshatriya by caste, had much to lose. Poulmani, a Chumar, the lowest of the low, had no place to go but up.

The little *ayah* was the most tireless of workers, and day by day her original timidity wore away. She had become a benevolent despot of the bungalow. Marjorie discovered to her pleasure that the *ayah's* small but powerful hands possessed to a remarkable degree the skill of Indian massage.

As Marjorie's pregnancy advanced, the *ayah* encouraged her to walk and exercise. Daily she would gently but firmly massage her mistress. And in the age-old way of Indian women she taught Marjorie the Eastern wisdom of childbearing, "When your child struggles to be born, do not resist its efforts. Let the waves of pain carry you along. Relax with them. Only when within you the waves retreat not, struggle. The time of birth has come."

Robert was not overly pleased at Poulmani's new role of medical adviser. But he did admit to his wife that in their own way the Indian women had been practicing the comparatively new Western method of natural childbirth for generations. And he offered no strenuous objections as he saw Marjorie practicing her exercises of relaxation painstakingly. If it did nothing more than stimulate her to a healthy and happy frame of mind, it was worthwhile.

When Mohardas the *punkha walla* came to his study with a note, carefully written on a scrap of paper with an Indian quill pen — professionally, no doubt, by the village letter writer — requesting that he and his wife eat with the undersigned, Robert's first inclination was to refuse this dinner in honor of the *punkha walla's* savior. But on second thought this trip of honor, too, might be of therapeutic value for Marjorie. Ever since he had had to disappoint Marjorie in his promise to take her to the States for the birth of the baby, he had been unusually solicitous to make good her disappointment in other ways. And so he wrote instead an acceptance.

The *punkha walla's* parents lived in a village across the Weeping River, and since the boy's father was the head *mahout* at the palace, they would be making the trip by elephant. It was a lovely September day when the elephant arrived for their outing. After the rains stopped, usually in July, the whole countryside bloomed lavishly through the months until early in March the parched dry breath of the hot season once again withered life away. Today the fragrance of myriads of open blossoms filled the air. The borrowed elephant himself was garlanded with a dozen leis made from the fragrant jasmine.

The *mahout* bowed as he placed the leis prepared for Robert and Marjorie about their necks. Robert had long since ceased to feel the wearing of these garlands effeminate. Marjorie was enthusiastic over the elephant, the *mahout's* attentions, the lovely flowers. Robert had not seen his wife so happy in months. What he did not realize was that the primary reason for the bright sparkle in her eyes was the anticipation of a day alone with him.

"Mounting the elephant is an art. Etiquette permits one to mount fore or aft," Robert explained.

The *mahout* gave the royal beast a command in a special elephant language. With a clumsy grace, the two huge front feet bent out at the knees, and the two back ones knelt, bringing the mammoth animal to a level position.

Robert had not yet learned to climb on from the front by way of the twisted trunk, holding to both big ears and vaulting over the tiny eyes. He preferred to climb up by way of the tail. This the *mahout* twisted to form the first step. Then clinging to the ropes of the *howda* Robert pulled himself to the top.

With respect for the condition of the guest of honor the *mahout* produced from the side of the *howda*, where it had been securely tied, a bamboo ladder. Placing her feet on the middle rung, and giving her husband her hand, with a helpful and respectful push from the rear, Marjorie arrived at her place upon the cushions.

The *mahout* now went to the front of the elephant and gave a command. Obediently the big beast curled and held his trunk out so that Mohardas walked slowly up, as if climbing a tree, and took his place on the thick wrinkled neck. His father gravely followed him and set himself down behind the big ears.

As the driver called, *"Oot! Oot!"* Robert put an arm about Marjorie to steady her. Both front legs of the elephant came up at once, and the *howda* hung back perilously at a ninety degree angle. They were thrown back against the pillows. Then the two rear legs lifted themselves and they were upright again.

Poulmani called out her good-bys and fussed along on foot to the gates, giving her final instructions to Robert about the Memsahib's care.

"Poulmani," smiled Robert, "does not feel I am qualified to take care of you."

Marjorie returned his smile. It felt good to have the spirit of comradeship with Robert in some measure restored. They waved to Charis as their animal swayed past the hospital. From there it carefully slid its great bulk down to the bed of the Weeping River. It took all of a half hour to cross the stream. Before every step it took, the elephant let down its trunk and felt about for a sandy spot on which to allow its big leg to settle with safety.

"The elephant is the most cautious of all animals, and the safest to ride," Robert explained. "He is testing the river for quicksand. He will cross only where it is safe."

And so they zigzagged slowly over the Weeping River. At times the stream reached to the level of the first rung of the *howda,* and when it did the beast turned itself to face the current, maneuvering itself through the deep waters as skillfully as any fragile canoe.

There was a short ride after they had navigated the river through the jungle before the *pahara* of the *punkha walla* was reached. The elephant had a strange gait; unlike a horse, it moved the two legs on the same side simultaneously, then the two on the other side. The movement of the *howda* was almost that of a cradle. And while Marjorie leaned back against the cushions she could understand why Robert, usually so cautious, had not denied her the pleasure of this trip. It was relaxing and safe.

Some of the branches under which the elephant went were so low they brushed the roof of the canopy above them. They could see the lovely bright plumage of strange birds, who scorned flight as their jungle paradise was invaded, and who screeched instead their contempt in noisy, unlovely voices.

At moments it seemed in the distance that the jungle was aflame. Then as they drew nearer they saw that some trees were ablaze with their own color. Their leaves were the flames. These were the well-known flame of the forest trees.

Marjorie leaned back against the *howda,* conscious of the long limbed husband who stretched out beside her, and of his supporting arm. Too soon for her they arrived at a jungle clearing where a half dozen mud huts clustered together like mushrooms. The whole village, and no doubt many visitors from miles inland, were there to greet them. More garlands were brought and placed about their necks, and they were led to a bed in the center of the square. It was their couch of honor.

They listened in silence to a long speech which was given by what was obviously the headman of the village. "They are praising you, Marjorie, for what you did for Mohardas, the son of this village. Have you any reply you want me to give them?" Robert bent toward her.

Marjorie had only heard catches of phrases which she could understand, for the bulk of the speech had been in the native dialect. As Robert turned to her now she hung her head, "I am ashamed, Robert. You know how little heroism I really displayed."

Robert looked gravely at his wife, then turned to the people and spoke a few words. They smiled and nodded their heads, "yes" in agreement. It was a courtesy they always accorded a speaker regardless of how they really felt. The man who was their chief spokesman kept saying, "*Sucha bat. Sucha bat* (It is true. It is true.)."

Robert finished, sat down, and himself led the applause in the Indian manner.

"What did you tell them?" his wife asked.

"I told them we did not want to speak of what you had done. Rather I wanted to tell them the story of another who had died for them."

"Is the old man who agreed so emphatically a believer?"

"No, he is just assigned to be the Amen man. If I said the world is made of green cheese, he would repeat just as vigorously, '*Sucha bat; sucha bat.* It is true; it is true.'"

The *mahout* led them at the conclusion of these opening exercises to a freshly swept courtyard. The cow manure which had been waxed over the surface had hardened into a pavement of concentric circles, into a pretty design. They walked across this ornate yard and into the one-room house. A bed had again been placed here in the middle of the room. Marjorie was led to it. Robert smiled his refusal, and sat instead cross-legged like a native on the floor.

A smiling woman with a large ring in her nose came and

brought a large cup of water and holding a basin deftly with the one hand, went first to Robert and then to Marjorie that they might wash their hands. Robert exchanged an amused glance with his wife at this deference paid to the man of the house.

This ceremony completed, heaping brass plates of curry and rice were brought in by their hostess. Robert thanked her as he took a generous serving. Marjorie prayed fervently for a "missionary stomach," when to her surprise, with much pride and laughter she was proffered a *lota* of soup. As she bent over the steaming bowl, the hostess with a broad smile came back from the kitchen and pointed to the can from which it had come. It had been especially ordered for her. Good American soup! She joined in fervently as Robert gave thanks.

Robert skillfully took his right hand and using the thumb as a projector flicked a palmful of the savory currybhat into his mouth. He explained as he did so to Marjorie, "Saliva is abhorrent to the Hindu; fingers must never touch the lips when you eat with your hands. Our custom of dipping a utensil into the dish, taking it deep into our mouths, and then reusing it in the food causes even the most casual of them to shudder."

For a moment Marjorie puzzled over how to manage her own soup. Then watching her host pour water skillfully from the *lota* into his mouth without his lips touching the vessel, she started apprehensively to raise her cup. The hostess gently touched her arm and handed her a soup spoon. She was hard put to restrain a laugh as her eyes caught Robert's. The defiling spoon was carefully engraved with her own initial. It had come from the bungalow; and the downcast eyes of Mohardas made her realize it was not procured, like the soup, especially for this occasion.

CHAPTER 31

WHEN THEY RETURNED AT DUSK, Poulmani clucked over Marjorie like a mother hen. But when she discovered that her charge had not been harmed by the adventure, she probed instead for each minute detail of the trip. It seemed strange to Marjorie, but this woman had never been across the Weeping River. Her whole life had been lived on this one bank. Now when she went to beat her clothes against the stones as she scoured them, she would have big news to share with her friends about the mysteries of the other bank.

The Weeping River loomed large in the life of the villagers of Surrak Annund. The Hindus bathed daily; the more devout ones even more often. Frequently one saw a devout Hindu performing his ablutions, profane and sacred, standing waist deep in the stream. Usually he would face the sun, and holding his *lota* high above his head he would let the water stream over him. Although the Ganges and its tributaries were the chief source of virtue, all rivers were an object of worship to the Hindu.

The village women, too, spent much time beside the stream. It was their community washtub. The pitifully few garments of the poor were pounded daily to pieces on the rocks. A woman who possessed only one sari would wash one end of it, then drape the cloth while still wet, about her body, and wash the other end.

For the Christian, also, life clustered about the Weeping River. The Christian women usually gathered at the river bank in the early morning hours. They had a special section where they would huddle together, and bathe and wash. Poulmani, in the new dignity with which her life had been invested since coming into ayahship, was usually the center of the chattering group.

"It will be a boy," she announced to her audience this morning.

"Are you sure?"

"I have seen her body in the bath," she replied with no embarrassment. "If it were to be a girlchild you know the memsahib would be thick as the trunk of a tree. She is still now, here" — she gestured to her waist — "as slender as a willow. The thickening is here." The women followed her every gesture.

"Will the child be white, do you think?"

Poulmani looked puzzled. "I do not know. But if it is born brown and turns white I shall let you know."

"Will the doctor sahib let you be there?"

"Naturally."

And so the jungle news sheet kept abreast of the news in the bungalow. And Poulmani emerged from obscurity to become a woman of note.

"I understand," said Robert, "that we are to have a son."

Marjorie looked up from her dinner plate.

"I had it," Robert paused dramatically, "straight from Dhunwa, who got it from his wife, who got it from another wife, who learned it by the river from Poulmani."

"Poulmani!" Charis interjected. "It does not seem like our shy flower to speak with authority."

"Poulmani, the *ayah*, is a new creature. Poulmani the despised is gone. She is now an authority on many subjects, especially medical! And she is the supreme authority, it seems, on the facts of my wife!"

"Why does she think it will be a boy?" asked Marjorie.

"Do you want me to list the medical or metaphysical reasons?" his voice challenged.

"Spare me!" said Charis with mock alarm.

"No, tell us, Robert," Marjorie coaxed.

"Well, it seems Memsahib was observed in her bath . . . ."

"Robert!"

"You mustn't mind, Marjorie," Charis said. "I still remember my father telling how shocked he was the first time the news came back to him that he was white all over. Naturally you are a great object of curiosity. I was not born here, you know. My mother went to the hospital in Burrapur." With her usual sensitivity she regretted her reference to her own birth which had resulted in the death of her mother. She hurried on. "Your child will be the very first white child to be born in Surrak

Annund. Many of the natives are sure we do not give birth to our children as they do."

"I am beginning to wish," interrupted Marjorie as she moved uneasily, "that they were right. I wish I could pick this one from a rose bush!"

Robert reached over and patted her hand, "With Charis and myself standing by, it will be almost as easy."

Marjorie was grateful for his gesture of affection. As her heart had turned Godward, it seemed in some miraculous way that Robert had changed toward her. But it was not in her nature to reply with anything other than a flippant, "Charis and you — and do not forget to invite reporter Poulmani to have a seat of honor at the birth of our boy."

CHAPTER 32

It was Poulmani who told Marjorie the Sahib was planning a hunt. She had seen him cleaning the guns. Interested in the project, Marjorie pushed aside the bead curtains that separated the duftar from the bedroom. Robert was on his knees carefully checking the ammunition.

"When will the hunt be held?" she asked as she watched.

"I have scheduled the beaters to come tomorrow. There is game in abundance, the natives tell me, in the jungle which starts at the edge of our mission clearing. I thought with any measure of success we could provide the refugees with a little meat."

"Will they eat it?"

"If I just shoot it, and don't touch it, they will. People of their own caste can carve it for them."

"But I thought every good Hindu was a vegetarian."

"The more orthodox are. As you know, they are afraid if they eat any flesh, they are guilty of cannibalism. Believing that the soul may return in the next life in some animal form they end logically with this position. But in Hinduism, too, you have a great many who are driven by their unorthodox stomachs to eat anything, including 'somebody's mother' — anything, that is, except cow meat."

"Why draw the line at cow meat?"

"If they were driven to that extreme they would prefer to eat human flesh. The cow is more sacred to them than man. And when you remember how close to starvation most of the people spend their lifetimes, it is not surprising to see them exalt to godhood that giver of so much food — milk, butter, cheese — the noble cow."

"Will the orthodox resent your gift of meat to the refugees?"

"They need food, protein especially."

SONG BY THE RIVER

"Yes, but will the Brahmins cause trouble?"

"They may. I am not purposely going out of my way to incite them. I feel this hunt is the humane thing to have."

"Robert, would you let me come along?"

When her husband raised his eyebrows, she rushed on, "You know I have never been on a hunt. You promised to take me some time. I would so love to go. And if I can still climb an elephant, surely I can still climb a tree."

He gave in reluctantly to her pleading. "It could be worked out, perhaps, if you wish. I will have the hunters make a *machan*, a hunting platform, for you on one of the trees. I usually prefer just to sit on a branch. But I do insist that Charis share your perch with you."

At dawn the next morning the entourage started walking into the forest. It was the first time Marjorie had ever penetrated beyond the cemetery boundary. As they passed its walls, Charis fell behind, and so they walked single file down the footpath. Robert led, Marjorie was in the middle, and last of all came Charis.

Robert beat the bushes ahead of him as he walked. "I am not shooing away the tigers," he called over his shoulder. "Right now the woods are full of game, and the tigers must all be well fed. You need only fear a hungry or a wounded tiger. I am making this rustling to drive away any snakes from our path. They sometimes like to sun on the hardened dust of the footpath. If you give them any gentlemanly warning they prefer to slide away."

Marjorie looked with interest at the terrain that bordered the jungle path. On either side was dense undergrowth, but the trees were scrubby and did not shut out the sun. It shone through, making the surroundings look like a large patchwork quilt with the predominant color that of gold.

The first indication the short procession had that the beaters had begun their work was a wild flurry of bird life that flew directly over their heads. Robert looked at his watch. "They are on time — how they can be so exact with no timepieces is pure jungle magic. We must hurry. We are late."

They were almost to the trees which had been prearranged for them to use for the hunt. The *machan* for the women was merely a rope bed turned upside down and tied securely to the fork of a tree. A ladder had been left hanging down from its side. Quickly Charis scaled it, and then turned to help. Marjorie, agile even now, followed her. Robert stayed until they were both safe, and then walked fifty feet and climbed to his own perch in the branch of another assigned tree.

The beaters were not professional men but villagers who were happy to be paid by any share of meat that was killed. The plan was for the men to make a semicircle, a halfmoon formation. The trees of the hunters were to be on a straight line drawn from moon point to moon point. The beaters were to start walking in, staying within arm's length of each other, until they finally closed in to where the hunters waited. Any game in the area would fly from their stamping feet and clubs right into the arms of the waiting hunters.

This was a practical hunt, not for the thrill of the chase, but a hunt for much-needed food; and the most efficient and least dangerous method to secure food was employed. More sportsmanlike methods were left to another day. The only danger involved would be one for the beaters if a stray tiger got caught in the human net. But even then he would flee away from the noise toward the better prepared hunters.

They could now hear the shouts of the beaters in the distance as they beat the ground with their clubs and sang and shouted rhythmically. They were closing in. Robert's rifle sounded first. The women could not see what he had shot. Charis took aim next, and neatly felled a big blue bull, a type of wild deer. Its meat alone would amply repay the beaters. They were fortunate. Sometimes several beats had to be held, and even the place for the hunt changed, before they had any success.

Charis was reloading her rifle when she heard Marjorie catch her breath. There breaking through the bushes was a long sleek striped tiger. It must have sensed their nearness, for instead of slipping by, it sank on its haunches and sat as quietly as a cat, looking furtively about it. Marjorie raised her rifle.

"Don't shoot!" cautioned Charis, whispering. "If you only wound it, it will turn on the unprepared and unarmed beaters. Let it pass."

"I want it," said Marjorie. "I won't miss."

Whether the soft whispers had reached him, or some atavistic sense spoke its warning, just as Marjorie aimed and fired, the beast moved. The bullet must have struck, for with a roar of rage the tiger disappeared into the bush.

SONG BY THE RIVER

Marjorie, not hesitating a moment, climbed down the ladder and walked over to examine the spot where the big cat had sat. "I must have hit it, Charis. Look! Here's a trail of blood."

"Marjorie! Come back!" Charis screamed down at her. "Don't you know enough not to try to track a wounded animal!"

There was no answer. Marjorie had disappeared into the thicket.

"Marjorie! Marjorie!" she called, as she too climbed hastily down from the *machan*.

In her anxiety for her charge, Charis forgot her own common sense and knowledge of the laws of jungle tracking. She blundered noisily into the bush after Marjorie. There were no signs of tiger or woman. It sounded as if the beaters were practically upon them. She tore apart another clump of underbrush, and to her relief sighted Marjorie. Hearing her crashing through, Marjorie turned, "I've lost its spoor . . . . Charis, look out!"

The warning came too late. From its hiding place behind her the tiger leaped. Charis went down face forward under the terrific impact of the brute's body and screamed in agony as she felt the strong jaws tear into her shoulder. She had enough sense not to move. Knowing that the tiger is like a cat in its habits, and if she stirred it would only bite and claw again, and play with her like a cat with a mouse, with a great effort of will she lay motionless; but she managed to call, "Get Robert. Run, get help!"

The rifle shot was so close the explosion deafened Charis. Still the teeth remained locked in her flesh. Again and again above her the rifle exploded.

"Let go! Let go!" The voice was the hysterical voice of a woman. It was not Robert shooting, but Marjorie who stood above her. Now with her bullets all gone, she heard her hit the beast, using the butt end of her gun as a club.

Charis felt the jaws mercifully open as the animal turned toward the attacker. "Run, Marjorie, run!" she screamed. But her warning was not necessary. She felt the animal collapse, a dead weight across her body.

She must have fainted, for when she looked up Robert was there and with his skillful surgeon's hands was cleaning and cauterizing the wound. Then she lost consciousness again. She remembered only flashes of the trip back to the bungalow.

She was lying on the *machan* bed, and the beaters were carrying her with great care.

Would she die? How bad was the wound? As unconsciousness again blanketed out all thought, she clutched out at one remaining emotion, "I want to live! I want to live!" It was not a demand to be spared from death, rather the voice of a surprised child who when given death, for which it has long coaxed, discovers it never really wanted it.

CHAPTER 33

THE CLEAN WHITE SHEETS of her hospital bed felt wonderful to Charis. And the calm face of Anugra, her friend, bending over her was all the assurance she needed. "You will be well again soon, Missahib. Doctor Sahib says so."

"I'm glad, Anugra Bai." And she was. She was! What a long dreary road she had walked before she had found this joy. It was as if she had had to undergo three severe shock treatments before she had recovered.

Her own attempt on her life was the first. It had shocked her and left her fleeing from death, and knowing she would never seek it again; but there was no turning to life, to seek it. The death of her friend, the good doctor, had shocked her into realizing her days and everyone's days were in the hands of God. "A Christian is immortal until his work is done," one saint of God had stated. She had learned this truth and had come home filled with the sense of obligation and the duty to live out her appointed time usefully. She had been discharging this obligation dutifully, but with no joy. Today when death clutched for her in the jungle, then let her go, her cure had been completed. She now found life not just a dusty trail, but a glory trail which would end in heaven. And there were joyous *dak-bungalows* — rest homes — where the weary and dusty traveler could find lodging. As usual, one of her favorite poets, had said it beautifully for her. "Oh world, I cannot hold thee close enough . . . ."

When Robert came to give her the tetanus preventive injections, she wanted to tell him her good news. But with his usual intuition he spoke first, "Yes, I know, you want to live." He smiled. "If I may quote a doctor friend of mine, 'For a woman who is always shouting about the glories of heaven, you put up an unearthly struggle to keep from going there!'"

"Robert!" she chided him.

"Charis!" he mocked her. "All the way home from the hunt, you kept screaming, 'I want to live! I want to live!'"

She flushed. He smiled at her and scrawled in his illegible writing which she had learned to read, "Prognosis good," and handed her the chart.

For most Christians the lesson to be learned was how to die. Charis had passed a harder course, one on how to live.

CHAPTER 34

How strangely the same incident affects different lives! For Robert, too, the encounter with the tiger brought its own revelation. When he heard the shot from the women's *machan*, and the bloodcurdling roar, his first reaction was one of anger that either of the women would deliberately endanger the beaters by risking the shot. When he heard Charis screaming his wife's name, he dropped down, horrified, from his tree and raced to the *machan*. It was empty.

He blundered madly after the two women into the bush. For one ghastly moment he thought when he found them that it was Marjorie who was pinned under the tiger. When he saw her standing unsteadily nearby, unharmed, a huge wave of relief swept over him. Even while he rebuked himself for his callousness, as he gave first aid to the wounded woman, he did not fail to realize that in the moment of choice there had been no hesitation in his heart.

It was a revelation. For many months now, although his relationship with his wife had been more relaxed, there had been no real warmth in his feelings. It was as if this incident took the lid from his heart and let him see what really lay deep within. He knew now that in spite of all his bitterness at Marjorie, and his contrasting admiration for Charis, he was and had always been in love with his own wife. The realization flooded him with relief.

Marjorie was semi-hysterical from the shock. She explained to him in spasmodic sentences, "Charis warned me not to shoot. But I was so sure I could not miss. So I shot! I shot! But I did not follow the tiger just to win him for a trophy. I was concerned about the beaters. I had to follow, Robert. Please believe me."

He tried to reassure her; but his main job was to help

the men with their emergency litter and Charis. Once he started the wounded woman on her way he was free to give his attention to his wife. He called one of the huskier men to him, and in the oriental manner by entwining their hands together, they made a chair of hands upon which Marjorie herself could sit, and thus they carried her also back to the mission.

The other beaters, more practical and nearer the pangs of hunger, stayed behind to rope and pole and carry back to the bungalow the game they had succeeded in shooting. When this strange procession reached the hospital, Robert assigned both women to hospital rooms. He ordered sedation for Marjorie and then spent his time attending to the one most needing his medical skill. Charis now taken care of, he entered the room in which he had placed Marjorie. The sedative had not yet had time to complete its work.

"Charis?" his wife turned her golden head on her pillow and asked the question.

"If no complications arise — and with booster shots given, none should — she will soon be herself again." He was glad to be able to reassure her.

"If she had died, I would have killed her."

"If she lives, you will have saved her."

She looked gratefully at him.

"That was a brave, though foolish thing for you to do, Marjorie, to walk right up to the beast before you shot. You could have remained in safety yourself, and fired from a safe distance."

For a moment Marjorie was tempted to let her husband think her a braver woman than she deserved; but then with her innate honesty she refused to take the credit.

"I could not shoot, Robert, from a safe distance. My hand was shaking too much. I had to practically rest my rifle against the tiger's head, or I might have shot Charis."

Robert could not suppress a chuckle even in this grim situation. "It was still a brave act."

"Robert, do you love Charis?"

Her husband was startled by her question. "No," he spoke firmly.

Marjorie pressed further, "Have you ever been in love with her?"

SONG BY THE RIVER   143

"No," he was glad he did not need to hesitate. "Why do you ask?"

"I have been afraid you were ever since that moment in the Indian hut when Charis lost the native child."

He sat down beside her, and took her hand. He felt an explanation was due her. "There have been moments when I, too, have thought so." Seeing her hurt face, he hurried on, "I only know that today when I thought for a few terrible moments that you were the victim, my heart became plain to me."

"I don't blame you, Robert. Charis has always been magnificent. And I have always been a total loss."

He did not contradict her. But he did say, "You have changed, Marjorie."

She told him then of her new spiritual experience, but added with a touch of the old self, "Do you think Charis is very wonderful, Robert?"

"I think without a doubt she is the most wonderful woman I have ever known. That, my dear, does not alter the fact that I am in love with you."

"Someday I want you to think me the most wonderful woman in the world," her voice was wistful.

"Subjectively I do already. Only when I am objective — "

"Robert, why must you always be so scientific — even in love?"

"You can't divorce the head from the heart."

"Please stop being objective for a moment," she interrupted. "Kiss me, Robert."

"Mmm," she murmured when he did, "there was nothing scientific about that!"

"On the contrary," Robert started to say, when she placed the palm of her hand firmly across his lips.

"By the way," her husband mumbled through her fingers, "a friend of yours was inquiring about your health." She took away her hand. "The Saddhu," he continued, speaking more clearly now. "He is one of your great admirers. He told me one day that you looked like a marigold, and that you did not walk, the wind bore you along. What he meant, translated into scientific syllables, of course, was that you have orange hair, and that you never walk, you always run."

"Robert, if you spent more time meditating and concentrating, fixing your attention on a spot on the end of your nose, do you think you could make up a pretty speech like that, all of your very own?"

He crossed his eyes and focused, "I can try."

"Stop! Spare me!" As they laughed together it seemed wonderful to share once more the gift of laughter.

He saw the shadow fall across her face as her mood changed and she asked seriously, "I am afraid to ask about the child."

"You need not worry, Marjorie. The baby's nervous system is not attached to yours . . . ." Seeing he had failed to answer the worry in her eyes, he asked, "What do you want to know, dear?"

"Robert, have I lost the child?"

He laughed as he pushed the wet curls from her little face. "Goose! You a doctor's wife! Look down! Can you see your toes? Then answer your own question. No, you have not miscarried, and your baby won't be born with stripes."

His voice became more grave as he continued, "I'm sorry that you have had to go through the experiences you have, but although they may leave their mark on you, dear, they will not mark the baby."

She sighed in relief. "Robert, are you still there?"

"Yes, dear."

"You seem to be floating away."

"It's the effect of the sedative. Don't fight it. It is you who will soon float away."

"On pink clouds?"

He did not need to answer; his wife was asleep.

CHAPTER 35

THERE WAS NEVER TIME to answer mail. If he waited for a spare moment Robert knew this distasteful task would never be accomplished, so doggedly he set apart a corner of the evening for this work. Many of the letters, fortunately, could be answered quickly, and it gave him unmixed pleasure to see the pile of correspondence dwindling. The next letter he picked up gave him a twinge of conscience. Here, where he had deliberately pigeonholed it months before at the very bottom of the pile, was the board inquiry regarding Charis' qualifications for missionary service.

He read through the questionnaire, and tonight with no hesitation he answered all the questions which had bothered him on his first reading of them. He gave Charis his recommendation without any reservations. As he folded the letter and sealed and stamped the envelope, he could not help but marvel at the changes of a few short months.

Charis had had a complete mental healing. He would no longer consider her a missionary risk. In a wonderful way his own house had been put in order. And yet it was no miracle, rather a commonplace occurrence experienced no doubt daily in countless Christian lives. Robert remembered friends who, without Christ, sought that will-o'-the-wisp, happiness, by shedding mate after mate with the seasons like so many discarded leaves. He sighed. There was much domestic upheaval about and he as a Christian would not escape life's problems or life's temptations, but with Christ's help would labor within the framework of marriage and its indissoluble bonds to find increased happiness. In every case, at least, contentment that God's revealed will was being obeyed was guaranteed, and Robert knew "godliness with contentment is great gain." If a Christian husband or wife observed the Christian disciplines so explicitly enjoined in Scripture, it would follow as night followed day, that he would learn the joy of the Christian.

In his own case Robert had not merely reached the goal of a passive contentment, but studied Christian attitudes had borne active fruit within his own home. He was happy. Robert was too much of a realist to feel that his domestic problems had dissolved overnight. There was a long road ahead, he knew, before he and Marjorie resolved all their problems. But they would be walking together hand in hand down the same road.

Marjorie would no doubt continue, like a highstrung filly, to shy away from anything that resembled an approach to deep thought. She had flashes of apparent erudition, but her knowledge, Robert knew, was superficial and intuitive rather than a result of an effort of study. Robert felt strongly that every Christian had a God-given duty to develop every facet of his personality. There was much potentiality in Marjorie that was going to waste. And any waste was a sin. But with the newly established sympathy between them, he hoped he could succeed in introducing her to some good books, to a treasury of good minds.

After he had cleaned up his last chore of correspondence, he still lingered in the study, and stimulated by this concern for his wife, he started to collect and arrange a shelf of books which he felt might both attract and edify his wife. He filled the shelf with tempting morsels of religious knowledge. He had always been a scholar at heart; knowledge had never had to entice him to be her servant. But Robert was blessed with the gift of understanding natures different from his own, and he was well aware in the case of his wife that she would have to be teased along the pathway.

He was pleased with the shelf which he designated in his own mind as Marjorie's. Now all he had to do was to wait for a propitious moment to introduce a sample to her. He read some of the titles: *Screwtape Letters; The Lion, the Witch and the Wardrobe* — by C. S. Lewis; *March of Eleven Men* by Mead; *Splendor of God* by Morrow; J. G. Paton's *Autobiography; Stop Looking and Listen* by Walsh, *Jonathan Edwards* by Winslow; *Beside the Bonnie Briar Bush* by MacLaren; *Once Over Lightly* by Feeney; *Twice Born Men* by Begbie. Some were the standard classics; some were written by contemporary authors. But all, he thought, should prove interesting to her.

Although it was late when he finished he decided to indulge in a shower in the semi-modern contraption he had constructed. He worked the soap up to a frothy lather and covered with the bubbles he turned on the tap anticipating the release of water from the tanks he had placed high above the level of the bathroom against the outside wall. He braced himself for the shock of the cold deluge, but the force of gravity failed and nothing happened. Not a drop dripped down. He hoped, morosely, that he was a better doctor than plumber.

With that accomplished patience his years of living in the Orient had almost taught him, he slithered into his bathrobe, and going outdoors, climbed up the ladder to the tanks to investigate. This time there was no plumbing failure. Tilak, the man responsible for filling up the tanks from the well, had neglected to do so.

With resignation he climbed down, stepped over the sleeping *chowkidar,* and back into the bathroom. He tipped the *surai.* There was only enough boiled water in the jug to serve for drinking purposes; so he toweled off the fragrant lather as best he could. The shirt of his best pajamas, while hanging on the line, had been chewed to bits by a hungry cow who evidently liked red. As he slipped into the trousers which she had so generously left to him, he was feeling his complacency begin to leave him.

Inanimate objects and their perversity were even more frustrating than human beings. As he slipped under the sheet which was the most covering he ever indulged in, even in this approach to winter weather, his wife stirred, threw an arm across his chest, then sniffed audibly. "You smell good."

He grunted. On the next furlough he was going to fill a trunk, if necessary, with some good masculine nonscented soap. But tonight he had to capitulate and go to sleep smelling like a lavender sachet.

CHAPTER 36

CHARIS COMBED HER HAIR before dinner. She swept it back from her face in the style that Marjorie had suggested to her. She looked critically at the face that emerged from its screen of hair. She fastened her Peter Pan collar with a turquoise broach of her mother's. She had missed the feminine touch in her life before, and the new Marjorie was applying it now with a heavy hand.

"Throw your head back when you walk. Think of yourself as attractive. Your thoughts will show through. You will be attractive. It's as simple as that."

Charis was dubious about this oversimplification of her own beauty problems. It hardly seemed possible that they could be cured by a magic formula. But Marjorie was right about the fact that one's walk always betrayed one's estimate of oneself. Charis had always felt unattractive, and she knew her carriage indicated the inferior opinion she had of herself. Her shoulders always hunched in and her head would sink down between the sheltering blades.

Marjorie was also right in feeling that Christian humility included within its scope a proper regard for one's self, a virtue in which Charis was totally lacking. Doggedly now she placed a book on her head and walked gingerly across the room. The book slid off with a thump. *Oh, well! The habits of a lifetime can hardly be remedied in a day. At least I have begun the process of metamorphosis.*

I have never had a young and beautiful friend, before, Charis thought. *I have always drawn back from pretty women and sought companionship with older ones whenever I could. I am enjoying this new friendship. Marjorie, the new Marjorie, is good for me. And she is fun to be with. I have not been blessed with the gift of easy laughter. But I am learning to smile — at least at myself!*

She took one last look into the mirror as she heard the dinner gong. *Until I met Marjorie, I never thought about the fact that beauty, too, is a talent, a gift from God which should be used for God's glory. A Christian should try to look beautiful.* Her face fell as she critically examined her eager, scrubbed face — *That is, as beautiful as possible.*

Marjorie, in her quarters, lifted her wedding dress gently from its box and shook out the folds. The glimmering satin shimmered as it caught the sunlight streaming through the windows. She took the lovely creation over to her dressing table and held it in front of herself as she pirouetted in front of the mirror. The effect was discouraging. Suspiciously she stretched the material to its limit at the waistline. Had she ever been that small? Would she ever be again? "I will be," she said with determination. "I'll wear it as soon as I can, if I have to wear it home from the hospital!" She went to the clothes closet and hung it in front of the two voluminous dresses which comprised her maternity wardrobe.

In the adjacent study she heard the rustle of paper. Robert must have returned from the hospital. She peered through the bead curtains and seeing him absorbed in the new mail order catalogue she decided not to interrupt. The Holy Bible and the mail order catalogue were the two most important books even in Robert's library.

Robert, not realizing that he had been observed, thumbed through the new catalogue and turned to the toy section. He quickly flipped the pages past the dolls, and concentrated on trains and tractors. He glanced furtively over his shoulder, then seeing no one, he guiltily turned back to the page on dolls. He was reading the blurb describing a golden haired doll which walked and talked. He had read that far when the tinkle of the bead curtains told him his privacy was being invaded. Quickly he closed the catalogue, but not before his equally quick wife had seen his interest.

"Robert," she chided, "don't tell me you are doubting Poulmani, the prophet!"

"A man never really expects to have a daughter, but I thought it best to be prepared!"

She leaned over his shoulder and turned the page. "It would

be wiser to concentrate on this section." It was full of teddy bears and cuddly foam rubber animals. "This is a strictly neuter page and safe."

She sauntered across the room to the shelf which her husband had recently rearranged. Idly she picked a book from the shelf. "*Screwtape Letters*," she read the title.

"By the way, I have assembled those books especially for your enjoyment, Marjorie." He spoke with a casualness he did not feel.

"So I can hold my own in table conversation?" she couldn't resist asking.

He ignored the thrust. "You have much latent ability, dear, that you are not developing. You told me once you wanted me to think you the most wonderful woman in the world. If you were serious in your desire, here is one way you can impress me. Do try to develop your mind. Why are you looking like that?"

"Your eyes, Robert. Have you ever noticed how your eyebrows talk?" She mimicked them with her own and scowled fiercely.

"Have you heard anything I said?"

"Mmm. They do. They do knit together . . . ."

Robert sighed and shrugged. How was it Mitchell had said it in his play? "Marriage is three parts love, and seven parts forgiveness of sins."

"Enfant terrible!" he said, not without affection.

"Robert, you were saying something about my exercising my mind, developing my personality . . . ."

"So you did hear me!"

"Forgive me, dear, if I didn't give you my undivided attention. But I anticipated your words."

"Anticipated?"

"Yes. You see you once drew a diagram." When he looked puzzled, she left the room. The bead curtains dropped in place behind her as she re-entered and handed him a crumpled piece of foolscap paper on which were three circles scrawled in his own handwriting.

Robert flushed. "When did you find these?"

"You can see they are well-thumbed. I've had them quite a while."

She went over and glanced over his shoulder. "There seems to be an awful lot of me to fill up. Now your circle . . . ."

Robert deliberately tore the paper into scraps. "You think I'm stuffy, don't you?"

Marjorie did not answer immediately. She opened her blue eyes wide then said with a bewitching smile, "I assume that was a rhetorical question?"

Robert laughed. "Well, my dear wife, stuffy or not, there is your shelf of books. Make of it what you will."

Marjorie gave her husband a sidelong glance, deliberately fluttered her dark eyelashes at him, and taking her slender index finger, went across the row of books. "Eenie, meenie, minie, moe . . . ." She pulled a book out and without looking at it tucked it under her arm.

"Aren't you even going to read the title?" Robert asked.

"*Stop Looking and Listen,*" she grimaced.

"Cheer up! You're off to a good start!"

CHAPTER 37

THE ORIENTAL BEAD CURTAINS TINKLED as they fell in place when Marjorie entered the dining room. Robert, as usual, was pumping up pressure in the kerosene lamp in the corner. It caught on the first try and blazed with light.

Dhunwa's uniform was spotless. As he served Marjorie a plateful of rice he coaxed, "Try a little curry tonight, Memsahib-ji? Very nice." He never gave up.

Marjorie groaned silently and capitulated, "Just a tablespoon, please." Dhunwa beamed. "Unconditional surrender," she said to no one in particular, but looked across the table to Robert to catch the look she wanted.

What a lovely evening, she thought. *Robert's lamp has lighted. I have made Dhunwa happy. Now if only Charis will not start on a book review* . . . .

"Robert," said Charis brightly, "have you read . . . ?"

We're off again! Marjorie gave a feline smile as she talked to herself, *But tonight I shall give them exactly five minutes before I take over. I think I shall make my announcement just before the rice pudding. Good timing. Then I shall be spared that horror.* She watched the little minute hand on her watch revolve. *Isn't it strange,* she thought, *how Robert, usually silent, when he does get wound up always talks in paragraphs.* He was in the middle of one and had just stopped for breath when the five minutes were up.

"Pardon me, Robert," she said.

"Did you say something, dear?"

"Is my hospital room ready?"

"Marjorie, are you sure?" Her husband looked diagnostically at her. "You know with a first baby one can easily be mistaken." "Besides," he went on calmly, "there will be plenty of time." He patted her hand professionally. "At least we won't have to leave before dessert." He turned back to Charis, "As I was saying . . . ."

"Rice pudding!" muttered Marjorie under her breath.

Surprised but tolerant at another interruption, Robert turned again to her, "Yes, it is nice pudding, dear."

Dhunwa beamed. "Yes, Memsahib-ji, very nice pudding. Thank you. Nice, everything nice."

Nothing has changed, thought Marjorie, *and yet everything has.* She looked at Charis and the opening verses of the fortieth Psalm came to her mind, "I waited patiently for the Lord; and He inclined unto me, and heard my cry. He brought me up also out of a horrible pit, out of the miry clay, and set my feet upon a rock, and established my goings. And He hath put a new song in my mouth, even praise unto our God."

Robert has claimed the promise, "Deliver us from evil." And I? For me the months have brought a true conversion, for I have found Him, "the rose of Sharon, the lily of the valleys." For me "the winter is past, the rain is over and gone; the flowers appear on the earth; the time of the singing of birds is come, and the voice of the turtle is heard in our land."

How right Dhunwa is, she thought. *Before, everything for me was rice. But now God is in the midst of us and it is "nice, everything nice."*